REDEMPTION

TRANS-CANADA KILLER SERIES
BOOK ONE

J E FRIEND

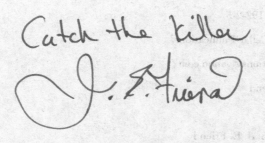

Catch the killer

Warning: violence, murder, blood, stabbing, drinking, smoking, sex, and reference to child predators

ISBN 978-1-9991192-2-5

Publisher: Dark Cellar Publications,

darkcellarpublications@yahoo.com

Author: J. E. Friend

www.jefriend.com

Cover photograph: J. E. Friend

Cover Designer: A. E. Hellstorm at Flying Elk Photography

http://www.flying-elk-photography.com/about-book-covers

❀ Created with Vellum

This book is for all truck drivers, who spend long hours away from their families in order to supply goods to the masses. For the drivers I met while I travelled the highways as I roughed out my ideas, who filled my head with stories of life on the road and for my husband Steve, who is also a truck driver, his love, faith and encouragement is what keeps me at the keyboard.

PROLOGUE

*B*rad Hopkins leaned back as he sat across the table from his young daughter and watched her finish the last of her milk with a satisfying slurp. He stifled a yawn behind his hand. After a full day of driving, he felt exhausted. The sensation had set in like a soft blanket of fog on a wet day. What Brad needed was some long-awaited sleep. He thought of the comfortable bed waiting for him back in his rig and struggled not to yawn again. One thing was for certain: no matter how tired he was, he wouldn't rush his little girl to finish her meal. Being a truck driver meant they spent too much time apart while he travelled the road. These trips they took together meant the world to them both. Still, he couldn't prevent himself from yawning again as he rolled his shoulders to loosen the tension in his neck. He looked into his daughter's eyes, noticing how heavy her eyelids were. For the first time, he realized she was as tired as he was and ready for bed. A last wave of exhaustion settled over him as he signalled to the server for the bill. While he paid for their dinner, there were two things he didn't know: One, before the night was over, he couldn't prevent the life-threatening injuries his little girl would sustain, and two, he'd be dead before it happened.

1

BRAD'S DAUGHTER slipped her hand into his as they left the restaurant. They were both oblivious to the devastation that lay ahead. The automatic doors swooshed open as they left the air-conditioned building to an immediate blast of humid night air that settled around them with a warm, damp embrace. Brad tightened his grip on his daughter's hand as they stepped out onto the hot asphalt. The echoing 'beep beep' of a reversing semi in the distance and the pungent scent of diesel were familiar to them as they watched for traffic in the busy lot.

As they stepped off the curb, a large, unkempt man bumped into them. A foul, sour odour emanated from his unwashed body. It was clear the man had spent too many days on the road without stopping for a shower. Large black grease marks stained his well-worn clothing. His heavy stomach protruded like an unrestrained balloon over his waistband, leaving a gap between where his shirt and pants met, exposing pale, stretched flesh over a large metal belt buckle emblazoned with the word 'Mack'.

Without apologizing, he crouched down until he was eye level with Brad's daughter. Repulsed, and a little terrified, she stepped back and pressed against her father, burying her face into his shirt. Brad felt her body tremble against his.

"Well, hello, pretty lady," the man croaked. A raspy sound, etched from many years of smoking, escaped from his lips. A foul, rancid odour expelled from his mouth, causing the young girl to wrinkle her nose in protest and bury her face deeper into her father's soft cotton shirt. She inhaled the aroma of clean laundry from the cool cotton.

The man scowled at her reaction to him before he stood. A sneer spread across his face as he pushed past Brad, giving him a slight shove, while mumbling, "stuck up little bitch" under his breath. Brad stumbled and shot the man a look of disdain before he wrapped his arms around his now sobbing daughter. Her body shook with each ragged breath, tears pooling in her eyes before escaping down her cheeks. Brad kissed her brow and wiped the tears from her eyes with his thumbs as the doors closed, separating them from the man.

"I'm sorry, pumpkin," Brad consoled, tucking a strand of her strawberry blonde hair behind her ear. "Some people just aren't nice. Forget about him, sweetie. Let's get back to the truck so I can read you a bedtime story."

She smiled through her tears, her chin still quivered as she lifted her head, her large jade eyes brimmed with the tears that still threatened to spill over. Brad reached out and adjusted one of the bright pink bows that held her curls back from her face. On it, her initials glittered in tiny black sequins, a stark contrast to the vibrant pink. He tweaked her upturned chin before taking a firm grasp of her hand to continue on.

They made their way along the perimeter of the lot, staying away from the constant flow of truck traffic. They continued on, unaware of the person who watched from the shadows. Brad kept a tight hold on his daughter's hand as she tugged on his arm, yanking him forward in a hurry to return to the safety of the truck and forget about the man. Brad made a deliberate decision to slow his steps, forcing her to slow down as well. He didn't want her to pull away, forever fearful of her getting hurt. When they reached his semi, Brad unlocked the door and helped her climb up in. She sat on the passenger seat, and waited as he removed her shoes, stowed them under the seat and instructed her to get ready for bed.

"I have to check the load, pumpkin; I'll lock the doors while I do. It won't take me but a minute, so when you've got your PJs on, grab the story you want me to read." Then he pushed the door closed and secured the lock before he slipped back out into the night.

When she heard the lock engage, she scrambled to the back to put on her pajamas. She slept on the lower bunk, and she left her pajamas folded on top of her pillow. She put her dirty clothes in the laundry bag as her dad had taught her, pulled out what she wanted to wear tomorrow, and placed the folded clothing on the foot of her bed. That way, her clothes would be ready for her in the morning.

When she finished, she slipped between the covers and reached under her pillow for her favourite book. She only brought a few with her. There wasn't much room for extras inside the truck, although she knew her dad would have made room for more if she asked. Then she propped her teddy bear in the corner and moved over so that her dad would have room to lie beside her while he read the story to her.

As she settled onto her bed, she felt the truck shift as her father stepped up and the door opened. He climbed up into the driver's seat and removed his shoes, but before he could close the door, she heard another man's voice. The truck shifted again as the man clambered up the steps, preventing the door from shutting. Her father spewed angry words at the man, words he never used in her presence, as he told the man to leave them alone. She saw the meaty hand that shot out towards her dad. A glimmer of metal caught the light before her father gasped.

Brad's face registered shock as the knife plunged into his chest and withdrew. In desperation, he tried to stop the flow of blood with his hands before he slumped over. The man stepped up, pushed Brad's body to the floor between the seats and slid in behind the wheel. The cabin light still shone brightly as he turned to her, licking his lips. Brad struggled to rise to protect his child even as he clung to life. Blood bloomed on his shirt and ran along the floor towards the bunk. Frustrated, the man thrust his knife back into Brad's chest, this time burying it up to the hilt. A tear formed in the corner of Brad's eyes as he looked back with a sense of helplessness at his terrified daughter, before they glazed over, lifeless.

The assailant glanced out the windows to ensure his actions were unobserved, knowing the cover of darkness served him well. He locked the door to the sound of her anguished screams. Then he shifted in the seat and stepped over her father's lifeless body as he moved to the bunk to the dimming of the interior lights.

The child's eyes widened in recognition. Her body shook, causing her bladder to release. The wetness spread across the mattress, soaking her pajamas. It was the man they'd bumped into as they left the restaurant. The air filled with the metallic scent of fresh blood, sweat, urine, unwashed body, and smoke. He approached the bunk in the darkened cab, stumbling over the body on the floor, guided to the back by the light of the moon.

The child tried to scream, her mouth opening and closing, but only a croak emitted through her teeth, which clenched as she bit down on the storybook she held. She squirmed back, pressing herself against the wall with the blankets pulled up to her chin to move away from him. She pushed herself further into the corner of the bottom bunk as the man finished climbing over her father's body, moving further into the truck. He loomed over her and folded the upper bed out of his way and secured it to the wall. He towered over her as his eyes narrowed to slits. His immense size filled the open space in the cab. In one quick movement, he reached out, grabbed her ankles, and yanked her down flat on the bed. She cried out, 'Daddy help! Daddy, please help me!', even though she knew her father couldn't help her.

Before she could scream again, the man slammed his fist into the side of her head and told her to shut up. The sudden burst of pain radiated through her as she struggled with consciousness. Her vision dimmed from the blinding pain and the immediate swelling of her eye. She kicked violently at him; but her legs tangled in the covers. His fist connected with her face again. This time blood spurted from her nose, and she choked as it trickled down her throat. She felt herself drift off, her brain fogging over, her mind slipping away from the circumstance surrounding her. She turned her head, with her one good eye, looked at her father's body, and into his non-seeing eyes as the sense of dread and helplessness filled her.

Her vision blurred with a mixture of blood and tears. Then the man moved over her, and his big, shiny belt buckle gleamed in the moonlight. She wanted to stop him from hurting her more, but couldn't move.

Her mind disassociated from her situation. Pain and nausea washed over her, now unable to prevent her eyes from closing.

The bunk sagged under the added weight as he climbed on, crushing her beneath him. Her every breath became more and more difficult. She tried to fight, but he pinned her arms, and her limbs felt like heavy molten lava. He hit her again to stop her feeble attempt to struggle. This time, he wrapped his hands around her throat and squeezed, observing her closed eyes, as her face changed to purple, swollen, bloody, and bruised. The pain dulled as she lost consciousness.

When he finished, he tore one of the pink barrettes from her hair, strands of her strawberry curls still caught in the clasp. A token keepsake to add to his growing collection. The man dropped the barrette into his shirt pocket before he stood up. He looked down at his blood-spattered hands and wiped them on the blanket, a mixture of the father's and daughter's, traces of which were buried deep beneath his nails.

He looked at the child he'd left, broken and discarded, then at the body on the floor. Satisfied that there were no witnesses, he broke the overhead light to prevent it from turning on when he opened the door to leave. Then he slid out of the truck and hurried back to his own rig, under the cover of darkness, keeping to the shadows. He'd have to leave and find another truck stop. It was now too dangerous to remain here. Someone would discover the bodies; the police would shut the place down and nobody would get in or out. He needed to be long gone before that happened.

With his engine roaring, he pulled out of the parking lot and continued down the road, putting distance between himself and the carnage he left behind.

WHEN RYAN WHEELED his rig into the truck stop, the sun was high in the sky and at full strength, glimmering across the hot asphalt in rippled waves. He drove around the perimeter of the lot until he found an empty spot. Ryan backed his semi in beside a green freight-liner and shut off the engine. He updated his logbook and slipped out of his rig, his feet making a soft thud as they hit the ground. His lanky frame cast a tall shadow on the pavement as he walked. He kept his strides long and even as he made his way to the building.

Ryan made a mental note of the different trucks in the lot as he went. He always wanted to know where other trucks parked in case he returned to find his damaged. His first stop was the restroom. Then he'd grab a coffee and a sandwich before getting back on the road. At 22, he was still new to trucking, but he loved it. For him, it was the freedom of the road. He was a bit of a loner and not having any ties at home made it the perfect career choice. When he entered the field, he'd considered all the options available before choosing to drive a flat deck for its higher mileage pay. He took pride in what he did, believing that a job worth doing was worth doing well. He always secured his load and delivered it on time.

With his coffee and sandwich in hand, he walked back to his truck, deciding to jog the last few meters in the blistering heat. Ryan reached up to unlock the door, then placed the cup in the cup holder and his sandwich on the floor between the seats. He started his vehicle and turned the air-conditioning on high. He'd only been inside the building for a short time, but the summer heat made the inside of the cab stifling. Ryan stepped back out onto the hot pavement and proceeded to his trailer to check the straps on his load. He wanted the inside of the truck to cool off from the July heat before he got back behind the wheel.

Ryan walked along the length of the trailer on the driver's side, checked each strap for signs of wear and tear, tightening them as he went. He continued around the rear and checked the lights before walking up to the passenger side, repeating the process. As he finished the passenger side of his truck, he paused by the driver's door of the truck parked next to him. Something wasn't right. He noticed there was blood on the steps. It wasn't fresh, but not that old either. He looked up, and that's when he noticed splatters of blood on the inside of the window.

His eyebrows drew together, confused by what he saw, trying to comprehend the reason for the blood. Ryan rubbed the dampness from the palms of his hands on his jeans, banged on the door and called out, 'Hey buddy, you, ok?' He knocked a second time without a response then he climbed up to peer inside. What he saw caused Ryan to step back and almost lose his balance. Inside, the driver lay in a tangled heap on the floor between the seats. Ryan could see that blood soaked his shirt, so he checked if the door was open. When he found it was, he pulled it open wide and leaned in.

Ryan reeled back as the sweet rotting odour of death mixed with the heavy metallic scent of blood assaulted his senses. His stomach rolled as he looked down at the driver's crimson-soaked shirt and vacant eyes. Ryan knew the man was dead. But he had to be sure. He checked for a pulse; his hand rested against the man's neck, noticing the waxy feel of the lifeless flesh. Out of the corner of his eye, he saw thin pale bare legs splayed on the bunk. He gagged; his mind faltered from the sight of the battered, bloody little girl.

Bile rose in his throat. He scrambled out of the truck, almost tripping in his haste. Unable to prevent it, he vomited on the pavement. He stood hunched over as he continued to gag and heave until his stomach was void of food.

Ryan wiped his mouth with the back of his hand, reached into his pocket for his cell phone, and dialled 911. The image of the broken child flashed through his thoughts as he explained to the operator what he'd found. The 911 operator asked him a few questions and told him to wait for the police to arrive.

He couldn't remove the horrifying image that shadowed from the back of his mind. His hand shook as he keyed in the number for his dispatch. He had to inform them about what he'd found and that it would delay him. They'd need to reset his delivery or switch out his load. His voice was still shaking as he explained what he'd found. The first thing his dispatcher asked him was if he was ok. His body tingled with the gratitude he felt for her concern. After reassuring her he was, he then asked if they could reschedule his delivery for another time. She told him not to worry, she'd take care of it. Now he stood back to wait for the police to give his statement.

In the distance, he heard the whirl of the sirens as he ended the call. He wanted to forget what he saw, but he couldn't. The image kept flashing through his mind like a slow-moving picture. Shaken, he took a long, deep breath to gain control of the emotions that overwhelmed him. He didn't trust himself to drive. Right now, he didn't care about his load. His dispatch would advise him what the new delivery time was. He slipped his phone into his pocket and stood close to his truck to wait and signal the EMS when they arrived. He no longer had the appetite for his coffee and sandwich, but he took a gulp from the cup of the cooling liquid to rid the taste of bile from his mouth.

Soon, emergency personnel flooded the parking lot. The flashing lights from the various vehicles signalled to bystanders that there was trouble. Ryan stepped out from beside his truck as they neared, in order to show to them which truck it was. Then he stood back as they cordoned off the area surrounding the rig next to him as the first officer stepped up to enter the cab.

Ryan mingled with the now-forming crowd, his hands jammed deep into his pockets, as he prepared for the horror that would play out when they removed the bodies. His mind flashed to the small battered body on the bunk. He squeezed his eyes shut, trying to clear the image from his brain.

He heard a sudden commotion coming from the truck and his eyes flew open. His jaw sagged when the officer came to the passenger door, holding the child wrapped in a blanket. He passed her down to a waiting officer and called out, 'Get her to the bus. This one is still alive!' The officer ran with her thin, limp, blanket-wrapped body to the nearby ambulance and handed her off to the paramedics.

Ryan reached out to grab onto the man standing next to him for support as his knees buckled. He cursed to himself. He should have checked on her. If he did, maybe she would have gotten the help she needed sooner. The 911 operator would have walked him through what he needed to do. He turned to where the EMSs worked frantically on the child as the doors closed and the ambulance sped off. Ryan swore to himself again for not checking. When he saw the condition she was in, he assumed she was dead, too.

"What about the other one?" The cop called up. The officer inside the cab shook his head.

"No, he's been dead for several hours. Looks like he bled out. We'll know more when we get him on the slab."

"Got an ID?"

The officer tossed the victim's wallet down. The cop on the ground sighed as he opened it and saw a picture of the victim. He was smiling, his arm around a woman with a child with strawberry blonde hair on his lap. It was the same child he assumed they'd just rushed to the hospital. He shook his head as he flipped through until he found the driver's license. It was always challenging to notify families of a crime, but more so when it involved a child. The police officer turned, spotted Ryan in front of the crowd, and signalled for him to come over. It was time to take his statement.

SEVERAL HOURS PASSED before Ryan could get back in his truck and head out to deliver his load for the new appointment time. It may have behooved him to spend the night and wait, but he preferred to head down the road to another truck stop, and put as much distance between himself and the grisly scene as he could. For as long as he drove, he'd never stop at that truck stop again. Memories of what he found would forever haunt him.

THE POLICE RELEASED Ryan because they didn't think he was their killer, but told him not to leave the country. The ashen look on his face said it all. Still, they had to be diligent. They took the time to check Ryan's logbook and contact his dispatcher to verify his whereabouts during the attack. Also, they knew most killers and pedophiles didn't call 911 and wait around for the police, although sometimes it happened.

NOW THAT THE body was off to the morgue, the investigation team combed through the cab and surrounding area, searching for whatever evidence they could find. Based on the man's driver's license, he was from out of the province, so they dispatched the local law enforcement to notify the family. The officers hoped that someone could get to the hospital before the child regained consciousness, if she did. It was hard to determine how extensive her injuries were before the EMSs whisked her away, but it didn't look good. If she survived, she'd have a long road to recovery.

HEADLINE - BODY FOUND

Police are investigating the death of a truck driver at a local truck stop early yesterday morning. The man, whose name is being withheld until notification of next of kin, was travelling with his eight-year-old daughter. The attacker left the child for dead. She is in hospital with life- threatening injuries and is receiving medical attention. If you have any information regarding this crime, please contact the police.

1

MAGGIE

*T*wenty Years Later

The crisp salt air whipped Maggie's hair across her face as she gazed out at the Strait of Georgia. She tucked the loose strands of hair behind her ears, slipped her ball cap on her head and lowered her sunglasses to shield her eyes from the sun's glare as the city of Vancouver loomed in the distance. She had her feet planted firmly on the ferry's deck, as she grasped onto the railing and leaned forward to gaze into the swirling depths of the Salish Sea. The trip from Victoria to Vancouver was a short one.

Passengers had just enough time to enjoy a meal and stretch their legs before the ferry docked again. There were two places to eat on board: the cafeteria, which was never Maggie's first choice, and a restaurant which served an excellent hot buffet. Her preference was always the buffet, as it offered a wide selection of food choices. Maggie could've taken the ferry from Nanaimo to Vancouver, which was closer to where she delivered on the island, but decided against it because she wanted to eat a hot meal that didn't come out of a microwave. There were few luxuries available on the road. As it was, she ate a lot of microwaved meals and felt she deserved something fresh once in a while. Of course, what she needed more than anything was a nap and a shower, but that would have to wait until she was on the mainland and parked for the night.

There were strict rules that passengers weren't able to remain in their vehicles and there wasn't anywhere else available where patrons could lie down and rest. She could lean back in a seat in one of the waiting areas, which she tried once, but all she got from that was a stiff neck, so instead she ate and walked the deck for exercise. When the boat anchored, at least, she didn't have far to drive before she could park for the night.

Maggie saw the dock looming in the distance when the PA system chimed, and the intercom broke the silence with a crackle, announcing that passengers could begin making their way back to their vehicles and prepare for docking. She smiled to herself, bent over, grabbed her bag, and slung it over her shoulder before heading back inside to the stairwell. Then she began the descent into the belly of the ship where the vehicle's hold was located. Her cowboy boots rang out with each step she took, echoing in the narrow stairwell. The sound of engines starting and the smell of exhaust assaulted her senses as she passed each set of doors leading to the different levels of the vehicle hold on her way down.

When she reached her level, she stepped out and made her way between the rows of parked cars, motorcycles, campers and transport trucks, before coming to hers. Big Red, as she liked to call her rig, was a metallic, candy apple red Kenworth 660. She circled the truck to do a quick visual inspection, including checking the kingpin to ensure that no one had messed with her fifth wheel lock, and then climbed up into her cab. She kicked off her boots, tucked them in the small space behind her seat before she slipped into her moccasins. It may be a truck, but it was also her home when she was on the road. Living in a small space meant she did everything she could to keep it clean. She went into the back and stowed her bag, then grabbed a Red Bull from the mini-fridge. She was dying for a cigarette, but she wouldn't light up in the boat's hull. Instead, she'd wait until they docked. In anticipation, she took one from the package and slipped it behind her ear.

THE PROCEDURE for disembarking from the ship was straightforward but tedious. Members of the ship's personnel stood at the front and directed each vehicle when it was time to move forward and depart. The vehicles moved in a slow, steady stream, but the process was time-consuming. She'd parked her truck at the halfway point in the hold and waited to move forward.

When her turn came, she maneuvered her rig out of the hold and onto dry land, following the slow-moving line of vehicles ahead. Once she was away from the dock, she rolled down her window and lit her cigarette. Inhaling deeply on the first drag, keeping it clenched between her lips, smoke curling into her eyes, she continued to wheel her way out of the port.

Maggie noted the time on the dash clock and breathed a sigh of relief; she missed the rush-hour traffic. She had little time remaining on her day, and she needed to make it to her destination before the clock ran out. An accident on the highway would mess up her schedule, but the snarl of rush hour traffic could be worse.

She continued onto Highway 1 as she headed to Chilliwack. It would have been easier to stay on the island and wait to pick up her load, but there was little truck parking available. So, she had offloaded the Audis at the Motorsports in Duncan and returned to the mainland. Now she had three days to sit and wait before she could return to the island. In Chilliwack, at least there was plenty to do, and the Husky was within walking distance of pretty much everything.

As a long-haul trucker, Maggie travelled from coast to coast many times. One thing was for sure, Canada was a beautiful country, but with the majestic mountain range it was hard not to appreciate BC. Still, it always disappointed her at the sharp contrast between the rich and the poor in Canada's warmest coastal region. She looked around and observed the trash that littered the highway between Vancouver and Chilliwack. Small shanties of homeless people spotted the wooded areas just off the road, impromptu lean-to's and tents dotted the landscape. It was a sad sight.

But Vancouver's central core was often worse. Downtown, long lines of downtrodden waited at soup kitchens and halfway houses for help. Nearby the convention centre, where displays of opulence contrasted the harsh reality outside. She understood why so many homeless people migrated here. On average, it was warmer in the winter than anywhere else in Canada. It was unfortunate the government couldn't do more for them. But the high cost of living here made it difficult to survive unless you had a good-paying job.

MAGGIE WATCHED as the majestic mountain range loomed in the distance. She loved the snow-capped peaks, even at the height of summer. Maggie passed an excessive amount of rubbish in the median. She wondered to herself if the West Coast had a disrespect for their environment or if the higher homeless rate caused so much discarded trash. It was then that she noticed a car ahead of her that swerved in and out of his lane. She slowed down to give him more room and avoid getting into a collision. She tried to determine why he was driving in such an erratic manner, and watched in horror as the driver leaned into the back of his car and reached for something. His vehicle slid to the right edge of the lane as he did. He popped his head up and straightened the wheel. Then he threw a pile of garbage out onto the highway. He repeated this several times as handful after handful of trash landed on the pavement, tumbling along the roadway and collecting on the grassy knolls on either side.

Maggie shook her head in disbelief. She checked his license plate and discovered it was from BC. She guessed the trashy roadside was a mixture of the homeless population and a disregard for nature and decency.

Up ahead, the exit sign for Chilliwack came into view. Maggie looked down at the time remaining on her day and breathed a small sigh of relief. Then she signalled her exit and pulled off the highway, making her way to the Husky Truck-stop.

Maggie wheeled her rig along the back row and found a spot in the lot's far rear corner. She preferred to park in the back of the lot.

It forced her to walk further to the washrooms and gave her some much-needed exercise after spending 13 hours behind the wheel. Plus, it was quieter, with less traffic. She found that most truckers wanted the spots closest to the bathrooms and diner, so those spots filled up first.

Soon, the others from the tour would arrive. At this point in the day, they'd find themselves parked all over the lot, but tomorrow, when the lot emptied, they'd move their rigs around in order to congregate together. That way, they could enjoy some friendly conversation and a little atypical tailgating. If the weather held out, they would socialize and BBQ in between the rigs. If not, they'd make use of one of the empty trailers.

She checked her mirrors before she backed into her spot and pulled the brake. Then she completed her driver's log, signed off, and began her reset. Not that long ago, drivers still used paper logs to record the day's miles. They took longer to complete, were easy to alter, so she guessed that was one advantage of the Electronic Log Devices or ELDs. She shut down her truck and grabbed the garbage bag from between her seats to dump in the bin on her way to the building. It was time for a walk to stretch her legs before she showered.

She looked up and noticed that the sky was overcast, but the weather was still pleasant as she made her way to the garbage bin. Maggie saw that there was a pile of bags just outside of the bin on the ground, but they didn't contain trash. Truckers left returnable bottles and cans for the homeless man, who came daily to collect them. It saved him from tearing apart garbage bags in the bin to search for items. She reached up to lift the top of the waste bin. As she did, the rancid odour of rotting food permeated the air. Her nose wrinkled in disgust as she threw her trash in and let the lid slam shut, wiping her hands on her jeans in case she touched anything. She'd stop in the washroom and wash her hands before her walk.

Out of the corner of her eye, Maggie caught sight of Noelle, a regular visitor to this truck stop. Anyone who'd ever been here knew who Noelle was. She rode past Maggie on her bicycle, her typical mode of transportation. Noelle was the local lot lizard, a trucker's term for a prostitute. As Noelle rode by, she bounced her bottom up and down in the air. It was her way to entice lonely truck drivers to ask for her 'company'.

As a constant fixture, she came by daily to provide company to any drivers who asked. She made her way from truck to truck, always beginning at the supper hour. When she found someone interested, she'd leave her bicycle fastened to the vehicle she was in.

Maggie gave Noelle a quick nod and continued on her walk. She knew Noelle would stay clear of where she parked. What Noelle did for a living was her own choice. It wouldn't have been Maggie's, but she didn't care how Noelle earned her money as long as she kept her distance.

While on her walk, she stopped at the local butcher's for some fresh meat for supper. On her way back, she saw the others from the tour had turned into the lot. Time to get the BBQ going. She planned to feed the masses tonight, masses of fellow co-drivers, that was.

2

NOELLE

*N*oelle rode her bicycle into the parking lot of The Husky truck stop. The first person her eyes fell on was Maggie, and she cursed under her breath. Maggie was about 50 feet away, tossing her trash in the garbage bins. Noelle had nothing against Maggie, but her presence at The Husky could put a hindrance on her earning ability. Noelle noticed Maggie hesitated, then nodded to her before she walked away. She nodded back, but stayed clear and made her way along the first row of trucks. She made a mental note to avoid the rear corner where she knew she'd find the red Kenworth belonging to Maggie, well aware of Maggie's preference in the back row.

In her line of work, she'd learned early to be cautious and aware of her surroundings. After all the years she'd serviced drivers, she knew offering her trade close to where a female driver parked wasn't good for business. Drivers who knew each other often congregated together, and they wanted no one to know they used the services of a hooker. Thus, she made a point of knowing where Maggie's rig was; and knew that her friends would be nearby. Even if one was a regular of hers, he'd want her to steer clear.

Noelle didn't have a problem avoiding the back row of trucks.

There were several others to choose from. She preferred to stick to the transient drivers, those that didn't frequent the Husky, and, of course, her regulars.

There was nothing wrong with Maggie. They were polite when they ran into each other. Maggie didn't look down her nose at her the way some others did. But it was best to be careful. She couldn't be sure if she worked the area near Maggie, whether the driver she approached was with anyone else or not. A new driver who approached her was fair game. She wondered how long they'd be here and hoped it wasn't long.

SHE CLEARED her mind of Maggie's presence and continued to ride around, displaying herself with pride. Noelle was here to work, so she peddled her bicycle in front of the first row of trucks, standing on the peddles to display her firm ass as an enticement. The leggings she wore helped emphasize her curves. Looking good and staying fit was an asset to her line of work. It enabled her to get the money she needed in order to survive and afford her own place. The more skanky girls commanded less money than she did for services rendered.

Noelle took pride in the fact that she was clean, kept her makeup fresh, and insisted her clients used condoms. There were no exceptions. In case the driver didn't have any, she kept a supply of them with her. She realized she could earn more in Vancouver, but she liked the truck drivers and the Husky was close to home. She paid for her small one-bedroom apartment on her own and was proud of it. The truckers she met were a friendly, although chatty, lot. Sometimes that's all they wanted was to have someone to talk to. Truckers had their own beds in the back, so there was privacy for negotiations and service. If the cops were lurking, someone signalled to her to let her know, and she'd ride off.

She made a point of not hooking up with just anyone. The driver had to be clean. A trucker sometimes called her over, smelling of foul body odour and stale food. If that happened, she'd refuse and move on. The thought of an unwashed man caused her to gag, and that wasn't good for business.

She kept her dark hair short so that she could shower, run her fingers through it and get back to work with little downtime. Her regulars appreciated how clean she was, which was something else that made her unique. She even worked out a deal at the Husky that allowed her to shower between clients if they weren't busy. She paid for the privilege, but she supplied her own towel and was sure to be quick. The showers were there for the drivers, not working girls. If the showers were busy, she'd head to the restroom with her handy package of baby wipes to freshen up, which did in a pinch.

She knew the truckers referred to her as a 'Lot-Lizard' behind her back. 'Lot-Lizard' because she worked in the parking lot. The name didn't bother her, but she preferred the term 'working girl.' In some countries, prostitution was legal. It should be here too, her body, her choice. Her work didn't hurt anyone. She didn't have any dependents, and she had a clean apartment all to herself. It may be small, but it was hers.

When she was halfway along the first row of trucks, she saw the lights of one of her regulars flash at her, signalling for her to join him. A smile crept across her lips.

'This looks like it's going to be a good night.' She thought as she rode over to his truck, taking the time to lock her bike to his bumper before she climbed in. Maggie's presence was long forgotten.

3

RYAN

Ryan wheeled his rig off the highway into the parking lot behind the Esso in Prawda, Manitoba. Thirteen hours of constant driving wore him out today. He was ready for bed, but first he wanted to get supper from Yogi's Picnic Basket next door before they closed. His freezer was stocked with meals that his wife made for him, but sometimes he wanted something fresh that wasn't reheated. He needed to use the bathroom and brush his teeth, anyway. The convenience store at this stop wouldn't be open at breakfast time, so he'd also grab a muffin while he was there.

It was still early in the day, so the parking lot was empty, but it would soon fill up. Ryan preferred to get up before dawn and make most of his drive during daylight hours whenever he could. Of course, that depended on his delivery and pickup times, but after over twenty years of driving, he had seniority and often got what he wanted in terms of loads. He preferred to stop prior to supper to ensure he found a parking spot no matter where he was, and getting an early start often meant less traffic on the road. For him, it was a win/win.

Before he went to the restaurant, he finished up his log, got his coffee pot ready for the morning, and grabbed his toothbrush and paste so he could brush his teeth before returning to his rig. He wouldn't shower here, but he'd be able to grab a shower at his first stop the next day.

With his toothbrush and paste tucked into his pocket, he hopped out of his cab and walked around his rig to check his load. He'd check it again in the morning, but if he noticed signs of wear on the straps, he could change them out tonight before it got dark. All he needed to do was to tighten one strap, and he was ready to go.

Ryan made his way across the dirty parking lot. Gravel crunched beneath his feet with every step. The wind swirled, creating clouds of dust that churned around him as he walked to the restaurant. His breath caught, forcing him to cover his mouth and nose against the assault. Once inside, he brushed off his shoes and nodded to the tiny woman behind the counter who didn't even bother to look up or acknowledge him, instead continued to stare at her phone.

Ryan shrugged his shoulders and continued past her. He stopped to wash his hands and face before going into the restaurant. It was earlier than the standard supper time, so he found the restaurant almost empty. There were customers at two other tables. He picked a table near the window. From that vantage, he could see anyone who approached from outside and still see the other diners. He enjoyed people watching to entertain himself.

The server was quick to approach and to take his order, so he looked around at the other occupants. At one table sat an elderly couple, who enjoyed separate bowls of soup and shared a sandwich. At the other, was a young family of travellers, mom, dad, and two young girls. One of the little girl's hair had a slight red tinge to it. Without warning, his thoughts went back to the gory scene he'd stumbled upon twenty years ago, which changed his life. He clenched his fist under the table to control the rage he felt. Ryan felt an urgent need to talk to his wife and children.

'*Krissy would calm him down,*' he thought as he pulled out his phone and selected his home number from favourites and placed the call.

Krissy answered on the second ring. "Hello?"

"Hi baby, I love you today." Ryan responded, allowing his fist to unfurl.

She chuckled and responded, "I love you today."

"How are the kids?"

"They're both fine. Daniel's upstairs finishing his homework, and Jessica is at Katie's house for a play date. Did you want to talk to Daniel?"

Ryan sighed, overcome with relief, knowing his family was ok.

"No, it's all right. I just wanted to check in and let you know I'm at the diner in Prawda waiting for my supper. I wanted to hear your voice."

"Did something happen, baby?" Krissy asked. Ryan could hear the concern in her tone.

Ryan lowered his voice so no one would overhear him.

"There's a little girl in the restaurant I'm at. She reminded me of the one I found when I first started trucking. You remember me telling you about it?"

"I could never forget," Krissy responded with a shudder.

"This child is with her parents and is safe. But it made me want to check that my family was ok."

"Don't worry, baby. We're all fine." She reassured.

"Thanks, sweetie. That's just what I needed to hear. Ok, I'll let you go. My supper arrived. Good night, I'll head to bed afterwards. I'll call you in the morning. I love you."

"Good night baby, I love you too."

Ryan smiled at the server as she handed him his food. Speaking with Krissy had put his mind at ease and his body relaxed. She had that way about her; nothing fazed her. It was one of the many things he loved about her. Out of the corner of his eye, he saw the father plant a kiss on his daughter's forehead as they got up to leave. This girl wasn't in danger. She wasn't the battered and bloody child he found so long ago; this child's family surrounded her. He continued watching them until they were in their car and had left the parking lot. Then he shook his head, trying to clear his mind from the horrible memory of that day, which, no matter how hard he tried, stayed forever hovering just beneath the surface.

With his mind cleared, he turned to his hot beef sandwich and fries and dug in with a hunger he didn't know he had, washing it down with an icy cola. By the time he'd finished, he was alone in the restaurant. So, he paid his bill, brushed his teeth, and headed back to his truck for the night.

After he locked his truck, he slipped under the covers of his bunk, kissed his fingertips, and touched them to the faces of his family pinned to the wall. He pulled out his phone and played a few games of solitaire before he nodded off to sleep.

4

FRANK

rank downshifted his Mack as he approached exit 145 in Quebec. His left knee throbbed as he pressed down on the clutch. Decades of driving, lack of exercise, not to mention his ever-expanding waistline, had weakened his knees and his pain was constant. He could retire, but the transient lifestyle held too much appeal. Frank liked his privacy and only allowed people to know what he wanted them to. He had a few old buddies on the road, but he kept to himself. Once, he had a wife, but she was long gone, and now he preferred the open road and lack of responsibility this life offered him. He had a small one-bedroom apartment in the city near his company's home terminal, but that was only because he needed a physical address for his license. Otherwise, he'd live out of his truck. His needs were minimal and anything of importance, he kept in the truck with him.

Because Frank spent most of his time in his truck, the interior looked well lived in. The Mack may be an older model, but it was his. He purchased it new, and over the years added some chrome and a new paint job, but it still ran well. The inside was messy and worn, but it was just the way he liked it. The inside cabin was small, just enough room to store his belongings and essentials. He didn't cook in his truck like some drivers did, but he had a microwave and a fridge to hold some food and drinks. He preferred to buy his meals on the road. Then they were always hot. He couldn't abide soggy, stale food. But he also kept a good supply of snacks handy in case he got hungry between meal stops.

Now that he was off the highway, he pulled into the Irving truck stop to grab a coffee from Tim Hortons. Frank parked his rig in the closest spot to The Tim's he could find, which tonight was the Cat Scale. He turned off the engine and hopped out. The Cat Scale wasn't a parking spot, but he assumed no one would want to weigh their load in the middle of the night. He considered grabbing fuel and a well-needed shower, but he couldn't stand the 'frogs.' At this spot, they made you feel like a criminal, leading you down a narrow hallway with keys to the showers, where the towels were threadbare, and a tip cup sat by the sink. You even had to ring for a staff member to unlock the door to let you out when you were done. No thank you, this place was a death trap. He would take a leak, then grab his coffee before he continued down the road.

He preferred to stop at Grey Rock for a shower. They may be half-French, but they'd speak to you in English. It would be just after dawn when he arrived. The lot would have emptied a bit, and he'd have no trouble finding a spot. Also, the showers would be available after the early rush.

FRANK GRABBED his coffee and a half dozen donuts from the Tim Hortons before heading back to his rig. Just as he figured, no one was waiting for him to move so they could weigh their truck. He climbed back into his cab, which pulled to the left under his weight, causing him to spill his coffee on the steering wheel as he got in. He used the hem of his shirt to wipe up the spill, ignoring how sticky the wheel was with the mixture of sweet coffee and years of grime. Frank tossed the donuts on the passenger seat, lifted the lid and grabbed one before he settled in and buckled his seatbelt. Then he started his engine, put the truck into gear, and made his way back to Highway 20 to continue east.

He found that the traffic was light as he merged onto the highway. The roads were quieter, which was why he preferred to drive at night. He'd been with his company for many years and it afforded him the ability to be picky about his loads. He picked ones that paid well and delivered at the end or start of his day.

After all of his years on the road, he could sleep through anything, which meant the constant traffic in the truck stop during the day didn't bother him. Plus, when he slept in the day, he avoided the lot-lizards who worked the truck stops. They came at night and were too long in the tooth for his taste.

He reached over to the now already half eaten box of doughnuts and grabbed another, enjoying the sweet sugar rush as he continued down the darkened highway. From time to time, the crackle of his CB broke the silence. He licked his fingers clean and reached up to stroke his collection of souvenirs, smiling as he went.

5

IGNACE, ONTARIO

*A*s the man exited the restaurant, he was unaware of the person who watched him from the shadows. Oblivious, he made his way back to his truck, his boots scuffing in a slow shuffle along the parking lot as he went. The loose gravel crunched under his feet. Under the cover of darkness, the watcher observed every nuance of his behaviour. From how he hitched his jeans up with his left hand, the waistband not making it over his ample stomach that protruded over the top. His grimy t-shirt didn't quite meet the edge of his jeans, exposing soft dimpled flesh. Even from this distance, his unkempt appearance was apparent. The observer could almost smell the man's need for a shower, even from far away.

In his right hand, the man carried the stereotypical trucker fare of 2 large bags of potato chips and a 2-litre bottle of pop. It didn't matter that he'd just finished an enormous meal at the restaurant inside. That was irrelevant. Long hours of driving created boredom and food broke the monotony. The man approached his cab, opened the driver's door, and placed the items inside on the floor. He didn't get into his truck, instead he paused and headed towards the back of the trailer. The watchful eyes knew what he was going to do. It didn't matter that he'd just walked past the washroom inside the convenience store before he made his purchases, or that there was ample opportunity to use it before he left the building. His kind didn't care. The world was his toilet. This was evident by the rank odour of urine that permeated the air and the many bottles filled with stale yellow waste that littered the side of the highway and parking lots along The Trans-Canada.

After a quick glance to ensure he was alone, he made his way around the back of the truck, unzipped his pants, and released a steady stream of steamy hot urine onto the pavement. As he did, he tilted his head back and looked up at the stars. The eyes that watched him never left their target, as the observer donned long, plastic veterinary gloves and a disposable rain poncho. One hand clutched a ceramic knife with a firm grasp. Using slow steps to approach the trucker from behind, the sound of footsteps obliterated by the rushing sound of urine as it splattered onto the gravel strewn pavement.

Gloved hands armed with the knife reached out and grabbed the driver by his hair, snapped his head further back, and exposed the soft, bloated skin of his neck. The sharp blade sliced through the flesh, cutting the driver's throat from ear to ear, a giant maw of red and gore exposed as the head fell back. Fresh warm blood coated the gloves, spurting outward as the heart pumped the last of his blood from the severed carotid artery. The victim was dead before he could clutch at his neck and attempt to stop the blood flow and close the wound. The hand released the man's hair and watched as blood seeped through the gash and stained the ratty t-shirt crimson.

His knees buckled beneath him. As the driver crumpled to the ground, his body made a soft thump. His face landed with a dull splat as it hit the fresh pool of urine. The blood mingled with the pale-yellow liquid.

There was a sense of satisfaction from the warm blood that coated the gloved hands, but there was no time to revel in the sensation. It sated the need to end this life. Then the killer bent and wiped the excess blood from the knife onto the back of the driver's t-shirt, tucking it away to use again at a later date. The gloves and poncho needed to be disposed of, an old plastic shopping bag hid their existence to be discarded miles away. A bare right hand slipped in and pulled something from the right front pocket of faded jeans. Pinched between the index finger and thumb was a small, pink, plastic child's hair clip. The assailant tossed it on the ground next to the body. Satisfied at a job well done, turned and walked away.

6

MAGGIE

*M*aggie leaned back in her seat, sipped her coffee and listened to her companion's chat. She crossed her legs at the ankles and stretched them out to one side. When she had arrived in Calgary, she spotted two other drivers from her company and felt a sense of relief at the opportunity to break the monotony of life on the road and spend some time with people she knew. Before she pulled the brakes, her phone pinged with a text as they invited her to join them inside.

With the winter chill out of her bones, she sat with them, happy for the distraction and companionship. Even though she enjoyed her solitude, she also enjoyed the camaraderie of the other drivers, but a single female alone on the highway still had to be leery about who she spent time with. It wasn't until she switched from refrigerated to car hauling that she found a new family on the road, one who accepted her as one of their own, right from the start.

Her two companions, Josh and Tom, were as different as night and day. Josh was younger and had the most enclosed car hauling experience. Tom was new to car hauling, but had decades of driving experience under his belt. Maggie and Tom often both looked to

Josh for advice, taking the sage of his wisdom to ensure they did their job as professionally as possible.

When she first started with the company, it surprised her to find that all the drivers worked together as a team. If one of them needed help, someone stayed and helped. When they were on a tour, they all worked together until they loaded or unloaded every trailer. That way, if anyone had difficulty, there was always someone available to help. It didn't matter whether it was a company driver or owner-operator; they took care of each other. It was something she appreciated in this male-dominated field. She was more than capable of doing her job. It was just nice to know that help was there if she needed it.

The three of them sat in the lounge with their hands wrapped around their coffee cups, warming them and chatting about their respective days. Tom was rambling about something that happened on the road when Maggie noticed Josh peering up at her from under his hat. When he caught her looking at him, he looked back down at his phone, then spoke.

"You're going to get me in trouble." He grumbled.

"How's that?" She asked.

"Little Momma asked who the blonde was that tagged me on Facebook!"

Tom broke out laughing and continued to smile at them, waiting to see how the scenario played out.

"What did you tell her?" Maggie asked as she took a sip of her coffee, trying to hide the smile that played on her lips as she watched Josh's face.

"I told her you were another driver. It doesn't help that you're cute and your Facebook status is single."

Maggie did not lose the humour of the situation, and burst out laughing.

"If it will help, I'll send her a message and tell her I'd never date a trucker. Everyone knows you can't trust them. Plus, you're too old for me." She smirked.

Josh glared at her and then laughed as well.

"I think she'll get it when she meets you. You're not all that cute in person." He sneered in jest.

"All kidding aside Josh, if it helps, I can change my status to 'in a relationship.' No one has to know it's with myself."

Unable to control himself any longer, Tom leaned back and laughed a deep, hearty laugh. Josh was almost old enough to be Maggie's father, and he, Maggie's grandfather.

"Josh! Why don't you let Little Momma know how young our Maggie is? She's more like a daughter. Tell momma she has nothing to worry about."

"A ball-busting daughter with teeth," Josh grumbled.

Maggie turned on her phone and brought up the Facebook app and switched her status to read "in a relationship".

"There, little Momma can now read I'm in a relationship. She'll settle down soon enough Josh."

Josh smiled at her.

Now that the teasing was over, and 'little momma's' worries eased, they settled in and continued chatting in the now almost empty lounge. Their laughter echoed through the deserted lobby.

This truck friendly mini-mall had an onsite restaurant, along with the stores that catered to truckers in the travel centre, which were now closed. Only the convenience store and bar remained open. The low drone of a country song drifted out through the doors of the bar anytime someone slipped out for a cigarette between drinks or to use the washrooms.

They continued to sit and joke with each other as they finished their coffees. Although she bruised his ego with the teasing, Josh wasn't ready to head back to the silence of his truck and the loneliness that followed. None of them were.

As they continued to banter back and forth, they noticed a woman approach them. Black kohl lined her eyes, hardening her appearance. She wore a coloured scarf wrapped around her head; her hair bound in it until she appeared bald. Over her shoulder, she carried a large, tattered hobo bag. The woman's oversized T-shirt slouched off one shoulder, and exposed a fuchsia bra strap. Her skirt was longer on one side and her underwear peeked out on the other.

Her sandalled feet were dusty from the parking lot and the sandals weren't appropriate footwear at this time of year. Tom gave Josh a nudge, so he'd look up.

It piqued Maggie's interest, and she turned towards her as the woman approached. Tom and Josh watched with interest. The conversation lulled with the woman's sudden arrival as they each noted her appearance. She chewed on the skin around her nails, her shoulders rolled over, and her eyes darted around as she prepared to speak.

"I can't find my boyfriend anywhere. Have you seen him?" She asked in a panic when she was a few feet from their table.

They stared at her and shook their heads. Josh scowled at her, and Tom blushed, trying to avoid eye contact.

"We don't know your 'boyfriend'. Maybe you should check the bar?" Josh retorted.

"I know he's here somewhere, but I can't seem to find him. I don't have my phone. Is it possible I could use one of your phones to call him? I don't even have to touch it. You can dial and put it on speaker." She pleaded.

The guys looked down at their respective phones, choosing to ignore her. Maggie hesitated, shot the men a look of displeasure, and offered to make the call. Both Josh and Tom peered up at her from under their hats. Maggie sensed they disagreed with her decision, but the woman needed help. It was cruel to ignore her.

"Here, I'll call him for you on my phone, with it on speaker. What's the number?" She shot a look at her companions to hold their tongues.

The woman rattled off the number, and Maggie keyed it in. As it rang, she placed the call on speaker.

A gruff voice answered. "Hello."

The woman leaned closer to the phone. "Hi, I'm here. I'll meet you in the store."

A smile broke across her face as she hiked her bag further up onto her shoulder. She thanked Maggie and turned to leave just as a burly man appeared from around the corner. He'd pulled his long grey hair back into a ponytail. His beard reached midway down his chest, ending at a point. He wore a pair of baggy blue jeans, a t-shirt, and a leather vest that was covered with patches as he strode out from where he waited.

"Oh, there you are!" she exclaimed as she saw him.

He looked at her in disgust and then turned to Maggie's group. "Did she use your phone to call me? I was sitting just over there!" Without waiting for a response, he shook his head as she joined him, and they left the building in a hurry.

The trio watched as the couple left, heading not to the parking lot, but to the area of motel rooms along the back corridor. Tom commented it was strange for them to use this seedy motel, considering the man appeared to be a trucker and had a bed in his truck, but said little more about it.

Tom yawned and looked at the time on his phone. It was getting late, and it was time to head back to their trucks. Maggie leaned back to stretch. The long day of driving had caught up with her. They gathered their belongings and left the building. Then they walked back to the parking lot.

They'd parked all of their trucks in different rows, but not far apart. The men walked Maggie to her rig first before heading off to their respective trucks. It wasn't necessary. Maggie insisted she could take care of herself, but it was just something they did. They agreed that the first one awake would message the others, and then they'd meet for breakfast before they left for their deliveries.

After saying goodnight, Maggie climbed into her cab and settled into her bunk without giving the woman and her 'boyfriend' another thought. She locked her doors and slept to the constant whiny burr of the auxiliary power unit or APU from the truck parked next to her.

TOM THOUGHT he was the first one up, and as agreed, he sent out a text to both Josh and Maggie saying he'd meet them inside in ten minutes.

Josh picked up his phone and squinted at the screen. His head dropped back onto his pillow before he heard the second ping, alerting him that Maggie had responded. He sighed and threw on his clothes, taking the time to make his bed before responding and heading inside.

Maggie was in the washroom getting cleaned up when Tom messaged. She chuckled, knowing Josh, who liked to sleep in, would grumble about the early hour. She ran a brush through her hair and pulled it back into a ponytail before she responded and stepped out to wait for the men.

The server had just signalled to Maggie and Tom to find a seat when Josh hurried past to the washroom. They chose a booth with a half-wall that separated it from the table next to them and waited for Josh to join them.

An older man sat at the table beside them. As soon as they sat down, the man turned and began engaging them in conversation. Soon Josh came in and nodded at the man before taking the seat beside Maggie. Following some general chit-chat, the man asked if any of them had a knock on their trucks last night.

The men shook their heads, and Maggie just smiled, attempting to ignore him, well aware of what he was implying. Not that she was immune to having the type of visitors he was referring to tap on her rig. She just didn't want to talk about it. Her truck didn't identify it as being operated by a female. Maggie chose not to engage in the conversation and pulled out her phone to check her email. She didn't agree with how some women earned their living, but she didn't inter-fere either and ignored the gossip.

The man whispered with a nod, "Look, that's her."

They looked up as the woman from last night entered the restau-rant. She'd smeared the black kohl that lined her eyes last night, but she still had the scarf wrapped around her head. This time, she'd pulled her skirt down to a longer, more respectable length. When she entered, she asked for a table for two.

The man next to Maggie gave her a nudge. That's when she real-ized it wasn't her 'boyfriend' she'd been looking for last night; it was her 'John'. Tom and Josh grinned at her as her face flushed with embarrassment.

Maggie turned in her seat to watch the woman, who seemed skittish and uneasy. She fussed with her bag, moving it from one side of her to the other before slinging it on the back of her chair. The woman watched the entrance, looking for her companion. When the server came to offer her a coffee, she refused to order, claiming she was waiting for someone. After a few minutes of nervous behaviour, she stood and walked to the washroom. When she returned, she'd wiped away the remnants of her smeared makeup and made herself more presentable.

She seemed surprised to find that her companion still hadn't arrived, but sat back down at her table and chewed her nails. Her eyes locked on the entrance. It wasn't long before the leather vested man joined her, fresh from the shower. His long damp hair pulled in a ponytail trailing down his back.

Maggie wondered if he'd taken the time for a shower. Why didn't she? He paid for a room. It must mean this working girl didn't plan on spending the night. This dive wouldn't offer free soap and shampoo, and her guess was the man didn't want to share his. Breakfast must have been part of the deal, though, even if showering wasn't. The man looked up and caught Maggie staring at him. He shifted his chair to avoid eye contact. He knew they knew. It was no wonder he seemed so disgusted that she'd borrowed a phone to find him last night.

Maggie turned her attention back to her friends, and the trio finished their breakfast without giving the working girl and her date another thought. The driver beside them continued to chat, throwing in a few raunchy jokes before he too had to leave. In the end, when they finished up their coffees, Tom offered to pick up the tab, knowing that in the future, they'd return the favour.

With their bellies full and charged up on coffee, they were ready to hit the road and start their day. Together, they stepped out into the bright sunshine, said their goodbyes and continued onto their appointed deliveries.

7

NOELLE

𝒩oelle shifted on the bunk, trying to get her bearings. The narrow bed left little room for her petite form with the trucker wedged in next to her. She exhaled. Another truck, another trucker. Then she remembered. This time, she'd hopped in for the ride to travel across Canada. She was eager to leave Chilliwack for a while and get a change of pace. The cops were lurking around, trying to catch her in action, and she planned to avoid being arrested for solicitation. She knew she'd always find a trucker to give her a lift in exchange for her favours. She'd long ago stopped caring and counting. Noelle couldn't recall what this one looked like, so she rolled over to check. She stared at the profile of his plump, jowly face and struggled to remember his name. It wasn't good for business if she didn't. She hoped it would come back to her when she saw his full face.

She glanced his way and noticed his mass. Snores rattled the bunk, echoing in the enclosed space. She sniffed the air. His breath was foul, but she could tell he was clean. She reached for her bag and pulled out a baby wipe to clean between her legs and under her arms. What was his name again? Oh yes, now she remembered Mark his name was Mark.

Mark promised they'd be able to stop for showers later today, at the Flying J in Headingley, Manitoba. He claimed to have lots of shower credits, so he'd spring for her to have one of her own and not have to share with him. It wasn't often a John covered the cost of her shower. His kindness was based on the close confines of the truck, but whatever the reason, she appreciated the gesture. The small interior of trucks made it unbearable if either of them smelled. Not that it bothered some drivers.

She tucked her dirty panties back in her purse. She could wash them out when she showered and slipped into yesterday's shorts and tee. After her shower, she'd change into her clean clothes. She ran a comb through her short dark hair; took her cosmetic bag to the front passenger seat and repaired the damage to her makeup. She reached over and grabbed Mark's cigarette pack from the dashboard, pulled one out, and lit it. She turned the key to open the window, allowing the stale air to escape as she exhaled smoke, watching it curl in small clouds before it drifted out of the window.

Mark shifted in his bunk, now sprawling so that his body took up the rest of the bed, stealing the warmth left behind by her body, farting as he did. Noelle gasped at the smell and took another deep drag from her cigarette, trying to mask the foul odour. She needed to pee, but she wouldn't leave the truck while he slept. Over the years Noelle learned to never leave her bag, even if you just had to pee. One time, a driver left her behind while she was inside peeing. When he left, he tossed her belongings out of his window. She had to run after them as they scattered along the highway's soft shoulder.

On the other side of that, by taking her bag, the driver might assume she wasn't coming back. So, she would cross her legs, wait and try to think about something else. She wasn't leaving without him. She wanted that shower, and he might change his mind if she wasn't there when he woke up. Noelle knew riders were against most company policies. Therefore, he was taking a chance by giving her a lift. She needed Mark to take her as far as he could. Finding another ride could take days. Men were always up for a freebee, but not giving a girl a ride.

When she left home, she only packed an extra-large purse, which housed all her travelling belongings, well aware that if she had to walk, anything bigger would hamper her. This wasn't the first time she'd travelled across Canada by hooking up with drivers. She only risked going across the country in the summer. The rest of the year was too cold. So, she stayed home in the winter, where the weather was warmer than in other areas of the country. Travelling in the summer also meant she didn't need to carry much. She could wash her thongs in the shower, and they dried under an air dryer. Anything else she could throw in with the trucker's laundry that she'd offer to do for him while he watched TV. Getting what she wanted meant getting creative.

Mark's alarm went off. The sound disturbed his sleep. He snorted, and the snoring stopped. He shifted on his bed and stretched. Noelle, her smoke long since tossed out the window, waited and watched. His eyes opened, and he saw her peering back at him from the front passenger seat.

"Mornin'," he grumbled before pushing himself into a seated position.

"Good morning." She purred.

He stood up and raised his arms, lifting his sizeable, swollen belly with them, revealing his small, semi-erect penis as he did. He grabbed his clothes off the foot of the bunk and got dressed.

"I have to take a wicked piss! And coffee, I need coffee."

"Me too," Noelle nodded in agreement.

She slipped on her shoes and grabbed her bag while she waited for him to get ready. Noelle needed to brush her teeth. They felt fuzzy, and her mouth tasted like stale cigarettes and beer. She noticed Mark grabbed his toothbrush and was thankful. Last night, neither of them had bothered with proper hygiene rituals. It was more about finding the best way to service him, which his ample stomach and small penis made difficult.

Once he began, it was soon over, but that's where the acting and ego-stroking started - telling him how wonderful he was and how satisfied she'd been. Crap, she couldn't remember the last time a John satisfied her.

She slipped out of the truck and walked beside him through the parking lot as they made their way into the building. Mark told her to meet him in the coffee shop when she finished. She went into the woman's washroom and peed, her aching bladder thankful for the release. Then she washed her hands and splashed some cool water on her face before running her wet hands through her hair, spiking up the top. She squeezed toothpaste on her brush and brushed her teeth and tongue, fighting with the automatic tap mechanism for the water so that she could rinse. Noelle surveyed herself in the mirror, making sure her clothing appeared clean, swiped on her deodorant and finished with a light spritz of perfume before heading out to wait for Mark.

She scanned the Tim Hortons. With no sign of him, she was worried that he'd left. Noelle looked at the row of trucks and spotted Mark's truck. A few minutes later, he emerged from the men's room.

"Let's get a coffee and get back on the road." He said to her.

He ordered a large triple-triple and a Farmer's breakfast meal and her medium black coffee and a multigrain bagel with cream cheese. When he paid, she was thankful. The idea of having to buy her food when she was giving away the sex would have eaten into her cash reserves, especially if she wanted to reach her destination, which was Nova Scotia, but Mark was only going as far as Napanee. He'd get her as far as that if he didn't leave her behind at another truck stop beforehand. From there, she'd need to find another ride east. Then, before summer ended, she'd have to start the trip back. She'd work the truck stops to build up her cash and grab a few rides before returning home to Chilliwack, B. C. Maybe she'd even catch up with a few of her regulars along the way.

When they were back in the truck, Mark turned on his E-log to cover the mandatory 15-minute wait. He sat eating his breakfast in silence, taking the occasional swig of coffee. When Mark finished, he stepped out of his truck and did a quick circle to ensure all the lights were working and the trailer doors locked. Satisfied, he climbed back into the driver's seat.

"We're off," he said while he lit a smoke from his package. He pulled forward, jerking the trailer to check that the kingpin was engaged. He explained to her why he did that. Mark told her that there were assholes who pulled the pins so that when truckers pulled forward, they'd drop the trailer. Doing this was a dangerous prank. Sometimes the trailer would drop right away. But other times it would disengage as the driver was making a turn or on the highway, sending the trailer into oncoming traffic and endangering others. A good driver always checked.

Noelle kept quiet while nibbling on her bagel. Although most drivers were talkers, she knew from experience that they wanted to talk on their own terms. They spoke about trucking, trucking issues, or other truckers. When he was ready for her to respond, she'd be there. Noelle would listen to him prattle about the industry she was all too familiar with.

He pulled out of the parking lot and they continued east on the Trans-Canada in silence. About an hour into their drive, the CB crackled, and a voice called out.

"Hey, Mark."

Mark grabbed the mic on his CB and pressed the talk button.

"Ya, buddy, what's up?"

"Did you hear about the body they found in Ignace last night?"

"No! What body?"

"Well, someone slashed a driver's throat! Left him lying in a puddle of his own piss!"

"Fuck off! How d'ja find that out?"

"It's been all over the radio this morning. But the cops aren't saying much. The driver who found him has been chattering about it on the CB. I thought I'd warn you in case you planned to stop there on your way through. I wouldn't, though. There are too many cops."

"Thanks, buddy. I'll make sure not to. Out."

"Where's Ignace?" Noelle questioned. Wondering if she looked ignorant, not knowing where it was. After what she'd heard, she didn't want to stop there, not if there was a killer in the area.

"Ignace is a hole in the wall in northern Ontario. The toilets are always backing up, and the coffee sucks. I never stop there, so you have nothing to worry about."

"It seems these days truckers have more to be worried about than us working girls do."

He shot her a look, and she regretted her outspokenness.

Settling back with her coffee, she removed her crumpled cigarette package and lighter from her bag, pulled out a smoke, and lit it before she leaned back to enjoy both the nicotine and caffeine.

It wasn't long before Mark started talking about trucks and all things trucking while she smiled and nodded at the right moments. She glanced up at the GPS and noted the distance they still had to travel until they reached Headingley. Noelle wondered if she should find a new ride after her shower, but knew she'd stick it out and stay with Mark.

She appreciated his cleanliness. He made sure she was clean too and didn't mind buying her food. The boring trucking talk she'd get with any driver. In this situation, the grass wasn't always greener!

8

RYAN

*R*yan awoke from a sound sleep, to a sudden bang and a jolt to his truck. It took a few minutes for him to remember where he was, then he remembered he was at the Robin's donuts in White River. He wasn't sure if he'd imagined or dreamed that his truck moved.

"What the fuck? God dammit, some asshole just hit me."

It was his first reaction to being jarred awake by the noise and movement. Ryan was sure that it felt like another truck struck him. He waited a minute to see if it happened again or if he heard someone moving around before he reached for his pants and then he felt the truck move again. He swung himself out of his bunk and peered through the curtains. No one was there. There wasn't a truck or person moving around. Ryan heard a clattering on the catwalk and thought that someone was on his rig. He stepped into his clothes and grabbed a flashlight to investigate.

He opened the door and scanned the length of his truck, and saw no one. Ryan slipped out and nudged the door closed, trying to avoid making a sound and alerting whoever was there. Ryan flicked on the flashlight and shined it under the truck and trailer. If someone was there, he'd see their feet. Even if they were hiding under the trailer, he'd find whoever it was. He saw no one.

He walked to the front of his cab and inspected it for damage, expecting to see a dent on the bumper. There wasn't a mark on his truck. Ryan scratched his head; he was certain he'd felt something.

In order to understand what happened, he circled the whole truck and trailer. He checked for evidence of tampering and ensured the straps on his load were still secure. Then he searched the cubbies on either side of the truck. Once he verified all his tools were still there, he grabbed his Johnson bar. This time, he locked both cubby doors; as he continued looking around the rig. He couldn't find anything to suggest that someone had hit him, or had messed with his rig.

When he finished his search, he did a quick jog across in front of the row of semis, Johnson bar gripped in his right hand. He checked between the rigs. No footprints were visible to suggest that someone was close to the trucks.

As he was about to climb back into his rig, he heard whispers. He turned towards the building. That's when he noticed a young couple sitting at the picnic table on the deck of the Robins Donuts, embracing. They'd piled their gear behind them and laid out two sleeping bags on the concrete pad. Ryan shook his head.

The disturbance he heard could have been from them, but he doubted it. They had settled into their spot. He couldn't imagine them messing around with the rigs and then spreading out their gear. He sensed they planned to spend the night out in the open. It would be a cold one for them. The temperature was only 4 degrees, even though it was early June.

He figured an animal had caused the disturbance. Maybe it was a small bear on his catwalk. One that was long gone before he got dressed. He climbed back into his truck, laid the Johnson bar on the floor by his seat, and got back into bed. He found it difficult to fall asleep again with his now heightened senses, so instead, he peered through the curtain on his egress door to monitor the young couple. It was better to be safe than sorry and this way he could ensure they didn't mess with the trucks.

The young man unfolded a cardboard sign and placed it on the picnic table. It read 'to wherever.' Ryan assumed they'd chosen to stay at the truck stop for a reason, and now he knew. They hoped a driver would give them a ride to anywhere but where they were. When he saw they'd settled into their respective sleeping bags, he closed the curtain, feeling like a peeping Tom, and once again tried to get back to sleep.

Now that the night was quiet again, he questioned if he'd felt the truck move at all. When it happened, he was sound asleep. He may have dreamed it, and that jerked him out of sleep. Ryan still thought he heard something, and he knew he felt his truck move, but whatever it was, was long gone. There was no sense worrying about it now.

He thought about it again as he was drifting off and realized it had to have been a fair-sized animal to have moved his truck. He wondered if he should warn the couple that a bear might be in the area, but when Ryan looked back out, he saw they'd zipped their sleeping bags up over their heads. So, he settled himself into bed and waited for sleep.

WHEN DAYLIGHT FILTERED through the dawn sky, Ryan found himself once again wide awake. He pulled on his clothing and made his bed. He rummaged through his travel bag and grabbed his toothbrush and paste, slipping them into his coat pocket before stepping out into the crisp morning air. Instead of heading inside the restaurant right away, he rechecked his truck in the sunshine to look for signs of damage. Satisfied, he made his way to the building.

As he walked up, he noticed the young couple was still there. They had their heads hidden under the flaps of their sleeping bags. All of their belongings remained untouched, including a guitar propped against the outside wall of the building. They were lucky no one had bothered with their stuff while they slept. Ryan continued inside and made a pit stop in the washroom before ordering a coffee to go.

Now that he had his coffee, he went back to his truck, turned his ELD status to on-duty, and completed his pre-trip before heading back east on Highway 17. He would then deliver his load. The load on his truck was scheduled to be delivered into Toronto. Once he unloaded, he had a few days off to be with his family. Something he was very much looking forward to.

9

FRANK

Frank wheeled his Mack truck into the parking lot at The Grey Rock in Edmundston, New Brunswick. It was time to fuel up. He carried a load of produce on his trailer, and was required to control the climate on his refrigerated trailer or reefer to keep it from spoiling. If it rotted on his watch, the company would claw back the cost out of his settlements, so he stayed on top of it to prevent that from happening. As it was, he worked too hard for his money to allow something avoidable to cost him. If the reefer ran out of fuel, the temperature would change, so he topped it up whenever he could.

The thing that annoyed him was that the company didn't fill the trailers with diesel before drivers picked them up, but there was nothing he could do about it. His complaints always fell on deaf ears. One thing was for sure; he wasn't getting stung on a load, any load.

He surveyed his truck with appreciation before he filled it. The truck was old, but his; and it was pre-emissions. This meant he didn't have the breakdowns the newer trucks did with their constant sensor issues. There were many advantages to running an older truck, and he was glad that he'd stuck with his Mack. Frank was proud of his old truck. He'd repainted it twice over the years, had the engine rebuilt, and now it was cream with maroon stripes.

His load of produce wasn't due to be delivered into Moncton until 6 a.m. the following day. There was lots of time, so he figured he'd park and grab something to eat before he headed down the road to find a closer parking spot. The Caledonia truck stop was only a short distance from his delivery. If it was full, he'd find a spot on the road. But he wasn't worried. He had plenty of time.

He swung his ample frame out of the cab and began fuelling. While the tank was filling, he debated whether he should grab a shower. It had been a couple of days since his last one. He spilt some fuel on his hand and wiped it on his jeans. The fabric felt stiff under his fingers. Frank realized just how dirty he was and decided he'd better shower before he ate. He checked his watch. It was still early, so there wouldn't be a wait. It was a good thing he avoided the morning rush. When he finished fuelling, he'd park his rig, grab his shower bag and go inside.

NOW THAT HE was clean and fed, Frank went back to his truck. He climbed up and tossed his bag in the back, not caring where it landed. He pulled out his log, turned it back on, and then fired up the engine. Before putting it in gear, he reached up and fingered the cord of souvenirs. As his fingers brushed against each one, he visualized the circumstances of the events that lead to him gaining them. A smile played on his lips. It was time to find another. It always took a while before the right circumstance and opportunity presented itself. This time, he'd wait until he was on the West Coast.

It had been a while since he'd gathered one there. He grabbed his ape shifter, a set of brass knuckles fitted on top, and shifted into gear, maneuvering out of the parking lot and back onto the highway. These days it was getting harder to find the right souvenir, but patience prevailed, and when he saw the perfect addition to his collection, he'd know.

His life was on the road. There was no one waiting for him at home. His ex-wife only stayed with him for a few months. She didn't enjoy having a husband gone more than he was home. He'd only married her so that there would be someone to clean his laundry and cook for him when he made it home. He didn't want kids, and she did. So, he told her to get out, and she was happy to oblige. It was the best choice for both of them. He preferred the open road and vagabond lifestyle, no commitments or ties. He stroked his long grey beard as he waited to turn out of the parking lot. Yes, this life suited him well.

10

DR. COLEMAN

*a*udrey started her day early and entered her office almost two hours before her first scheduled appointment. After she'd watched the news last night, something bothered her. She wasn't sure what, but she wanted to review her case files before she saw her first client, hoping to find the answers she was looking for.

The news reported a murdered truck driver in northern Ontario. This wasn't unusual. The transient lifestyle attracted many dangers, but something felt familiar about it. She knew this wasn't the first time they had found a trucker murdered in recent years, but it was the first time she paid attention. The reporters had just linked the cases together, hinting of a serial killer, which meant the police had also connected the facts that the killings were the work of a serial killer. She had a niggling feeling that she could connect these murders to one of her previous case files.

She tossed her jacket on a chair and flicked on the desk lamp, not bothering with the overhead florescence. Audrey didn't want to call attention to her presence in the office. She worked alone, but sometimes when people knew she was there outside of office hours, they liked to stop in for a chat, so she made do with the dim desk light. She pulled her keys out of her pocket and unlocked her filing cabinet. The file she was looking for wasn't from a current case, so it was the cabinet full of past cases she concentrated on.

During her years as a psychiatrist, Audrey had counselled a few people who had suffered from a trauma that centred around the trucking industry. The information that the killer used a knife in these killings interested her. It was the clue that connected it to one of her cases. She was sure of it. Her hand hovered over the bulging file of news clippings that she'd collected. The recent articles she clipped from the paper needed to be added, so she pulled out the file.

Over the years, she'd gathered information and articles, hoping to put an end to the horror that haunted her daily existence. A crime she couldn't solve, one the police called 'a cold case'. It didn't matter how long ago it happened; it wasn't cold to her. The pain of it affected every decision she made. She continued to look for clues to help her end the pain.

She added the new articles to the file and stuffed it in the back of the cabinet, almost hidden from view. Then she pulled out three others. These were clients she'd worked with before where the trucking industry came up during therapy. She flipped through the files, checking her notes, trying to get a better understanding of what was bothering her.

She turned to case 156, then Audrey found what she was looking for. A reference to a knife. Audrey wondered if the perpetrator of the current string of murders was the same one described by her client. She pulled out some audio tapes from the early sessions to review. She hoped when she did, she'd understand what was bothering her and get some answers.

Doctor-patient confidentiality prevented her from contacting the police, not that she had anything to divulge to help with their search. Her client was a victim who needed to be protected, not a killer. A quick conversation could ease her concerns. At the least, she could check on how 156 was managing. It had been a while since they last spoke.

Audrey leaned back in her chair, slipped the first tape into the player, and listened to the frightened voice of 156 from so many years ago.

11

MAGGIE

*M*aggie listened to the crackle from the CB, which was alive with chatter. Everyone was talking about the driver found dead in Ignace. Ok, not dead, murdered, as if that made any difference. Today someone had corrected her three times already. She wasn't concerned for herself. So far, all the murdered drivers were men. She wasn't a man, so there was nothing for her to worry about. She knew how dangerous the road was and being a woman didn't mean she wasn't a target. There were different predators she needed to be aware of. The fact was there were fewer female drivers than men, meant it could be a matter of availability and opportunity. She told the other drivers she felt she could take care of herself. Killers, from what she'd heard, had a type. She doubted her petite female frame fit the bill based on what she knew.

She switched the CB off and turned on her radio. Annoyed that the news was on when she did. Her hand was on the knob to change the channel when she heard the new announcement, "Canadian Designer Kills Lawyer Friend, in a fit of jealousy." Maggie couldn't believe it. The world was going to pot. She turned off her radio and continued to drive in silence.

She reached down to the cooler bag between the seats to pull out

54

another Red Bull. It was her second one today and her hand had a slight tremor. What she needed was some food, but she didn't have time to stop. Maybe not having the time to stop wasn't true. She didn't want to stop. She'd wait until she needed to pee before stopping. Then she'd grab something in the restaurant or something from her fridge. She tried to limit the number of times she stopped in the day to optimize her trip.

Maggie pulled open the tab on the can, tipped it to her lips, and allowed the cool jolting liquid to slide down her parched throat. She ran her fingers through her blonde hair, catching the cigarette she stored over her left ear. Freeing it, she placed it between her lips and lit it. As she did, she used her knee to steady the rig. She took a drag and guzzled down the rest of the Red Bull. Maggie tossed the empty can in the trash with the growing collection of empties. When she stopped, she'd have to remember to empty her garbage before it stank.

She flicked the CB back on at a low setting in case there was anything she needed to be aware of, when the static from her CB broke the silence again. This time it was JD, another driver from her company.

"Hey Maggie, how's it going? Are you planning on heading back to the yard?"

"I'm doing well, JD. You? Yup, I'll head back when I deliver. I have to stop in Ajax before turning my paperwork into the office. Then I'm off to Alliston for my next load."

"Things are good here. I just wanted to warn you that Adam's got a burr up his ass. Hondas on hold again, and they're scrambling for loads. Your Alliston load may not be ready. Take your time getting back. That way, they may release the cars before you get there."

"Will do, JD. Thanks for the heads up. Chat soon."

Maggie continued driving down the highway. With her window open, to allow the fresh air to filter into the cab and remove the smell of her cigarette smoke. She may be a smoker, but that didn't mean she wanted her truck to smell like stale cigarettes. She only smoked with the window open and kept a container of coffee grounds under her seat to absorb the odour.

The sun shone high in the sky on the beautiful spring day. She was past Ignace and the crime scene, and the long delay of 'rubber-neckers.' Maggie hoped the load waiting for her was to the East coast. Then she'd make the long overdue visit with her father. She'd adjust her route if she had to in order to make the stop in Cobden, Ontario.

Just as she was thinking this, her cell phone rang. The blue tooth kicked in, the screen lit up, and she saw it was her Uncle Bobbie. She hesitated before answering, knowing he'd lecture her for not stopping in the last time she'd been through town. Maggie braced herself and answered the call.

"Hi, Uncle."

"Hey, Mags. It's been a while."

Maggie rolled her eyes; thankful he couldn't see the gesture. It didn't matter how often she called. It was never often enough. Then she continued.

"Well, you know how the road is, Uncle Bobbie. I'm just heading back from Vancouver Island. My delivery was at the racetrack in Duncan. I couldn't leave until it was over, so I stayed put. Where are you?"

"Down in Windsor. Listen, Mags, your aunt and I were wondering if you had any time off coming up. We'd love to see you. It's been too long." Bobbie paused, waiting for her response.

"I know. I rarely get that way. But I'm hoping for a load east this time. I thought I'd stop in to visit with dad on my way back. I could visit with you for a day or two. Would that work?"

"You said that the last time you visited him. You hurt your aunt when the neighbours said you'd been up to see your dad but didn't stop in. Come on, Maggie, she's like a mother to you."

Maggie sighed; he was right. The problem was, she enjoyed being alone. When she was alone, there was no one to ask questions or butt into her business. In trucking, they only expected on-time deliveries. Whereas family members wanted more than she could give. Being able to be alone was why she trucked. Her dad and uncle were both truckers, and her aunt was one of the business's best mechanics. They knew the score and shouldn't lay the guilt trip on her. Maggie glanced at the phone's screen; sure her uncle could sense her guilt.

"Your right, Uncle Bobbie. Aunt Julie will be my first call when we're done. I'll make it a priority to visit on my way back. I promise that I'll let you know as soon as I can schedule some real holiday time. Maybe we can get some fishing in on Muskrat Lake."

"Ok, girl," he sighed. "I miss you too, you know."

"I miss you. Listen, I'm getting pulled in at the scale-up ahead. I'll call you when I know I'll be going through so we can set something up."

"Sure, kiddo. Talk soon. I love you."

"Love you too, bye."

'Crap,' she thought as she hung up the phone. *I love them, but I wish they'd just let me do my thing.*

She thought about the hoops she'd have to jump through to head east. Putting off a visit any longer would just cause more trouble and suspicion than she needed. She swallowed the lump that formed at the back of her throat and called the office. She hoped Adam had calmed down enough to do her a favour.

12

NOELLE

*M*ark had long since dropped her off and was back on his way west. She'd caught a few more rides with different drivers as she headed east and was now working at a new truck stop in Enfield, NS. Her appearance didn't impress the regular girl who worked the territory. They'd almost come to blows over Noelle's presence, but Noelle explained she was passing through and didn't mind working different hours. They ended up calling a truce.

The other girl enjoyed working in the late afternoon. Noelle assumed she was a mother and had kids at home. The arrangement suited her. She could work anytime. Noelle knew her look wasn't soft; the other girl, however, looked as if someone had ridden her hard and put her away wet. It was no wonder she didn't want Noelle working at the same truck stop. The girl couldn't afford to lose customers. Although judging by her customers, Noelle knew the girl had nothing to worry about; there was no way she'd service those clients. She may be a working girl, but she had standards. Noelle preferred working over the supper hour and later into the night. Sometimes, she'd get a free meal out of the deal by working during supper time, which wasn't so bad. Noelle enjoyed working at night because it often gave her a bed to sleep in.

The weather got colder, and she realized it was time to head home. The trip east had been her form of vacation, one she joked about as her work-cation. It was how Noelle could see Canada. She made enough to support herself, but not enough for travel. Noelle subleased her apartment back home for another month, so her costs were down and she had money in the bank.

One thing that happened while she was in NS was that the regular girl's business had increased, which was the real reason they called a truce. Whatever it was, who cared? They both made money, and that's what mattered. Taking clients from the regular girl was bad for business. Noelle was familiar with someone trying to take over. She'd face that back in Chilliwack. Not that it worried her. She was a regular fixture at the Husky. If Noelle found anyone working there when she returned, that girl would get her walking papers and her ass handed to her before she even knew what hit her.

NOELLE STOOD and inspected her face in the ladies' room mirror, adding some extra kohl around her eyes before feeling satisfied. She used her fingers to spike her black hair and surveyed the result. Yes, she looked good. Then Noelle slipped her hand into her bra and adjusted each breast until they sat in a better position, offering an unobstructed view of her cleavage. Satisfied, she slung her bag over her shoulder to leave. Her eyes were on the floor, and as she left, she collided with another woman.

Noelle's eye flew open in instant recognition. It was the female driver, Maggie, who she last saw in Chilliwack. It was obvious Maggie recognized her as well, but all she did was to mumble 'sorry' before she pushed past Noelle into the washroom.

Noelle hesitated, considered whether she should ask Maggie for a ride, then thought better of it. Maggie knew what Noelle did, and although Maggie was never rude to her, she wasn't friendly either. No, it was better if she found a willing bedmate to give her a lift west instead.

The temperature had dropped while she was inside and a cool

breeze hit her as she left the building; she rubbed her arms as she walked and considered digging out the thin jean jacket she brought with her. Summer was ending. It was time to head home. She surveyed the parking lot, taking the time to look up at the long line of trucks, and considered her best option before she headed to a red truck marked Erb. Noelle figured this one would head west. She knew they had a yard somewhere in Quebec. She may only cross a province or two, but it would help. Time to work on getting a ride home.

She strutted up to the truck in the now twilight, allowing her hips to sway. It never hurt to keep her options open. She made sure that other drivers would notice her. The driver was sitting in his seat of his cab when she rapped on his door. He checked her out, then rolled down the window.

"Can I help you?"

"Are you looking for some company?" She asked.

He hesitated for quite a while. Noelle assumed he wasn't interested and prepared to leave before he nodded, motioning for her to get in. Now she'd begin negotiations for a ride west in trade.

13

RYAN

*R*yan pulled into his home terminal and searched for a place to park his truck and trailer as he prepared for some much-needed home time. It didn't take long before he spotted one in the far back. It seemed everyone had returned to the yard at once. He couldn't remember the last time the yard was so full.

He swung his rig around and then squared it up to the spot, checked his mirrors, and backed in. When he was in position, he pulled the brake and turned off the engine. Then he climbed to the rear of the cab to gather his belongings.

With his gear slung over his shoulder, he locked the truck and made his way to the building to turn in his trip report. The company was excellent about giving him advances on his more extended trips, but the actual payout came after he handed in his paperwork, and they calculated all the drops and picks.

He couldn't have found a spot further from the office than he did. If he was overweight, he'd appreciate the exercise, but his frame was so thin he had trouble maintaining his weight as it was. The worst part was that he'd have to backtrack to find his car. They locked the compound after hours, but the drivers all had the code in order to leave finished paperwork and pick up their next load assignment.

He'd also use the bathroom before making the hour's drive from the terminal to home.

With his paperwork completed, he stepped back outside into the crisp fall air, strode across the dirt lot, hit the key fob, and the lights flashed as the doors of his car unlocked. He tossed his gear and dirty laundry in the back and started the engine. Ryan smiled at the thought of heading home for some much-needed time with his wife and kids. He'd been away for weeks and was going to spend his re-set with his family.

THE WEST COAST runs kept him away for weeks at a time. He missed his family while he was on the road, even though he talked to them every day. It wasn't the same. It kept them up-to-date with comings and goings, that was all.

This time, instead of the usual thirty-six hours at home, he was taking off four straight days. It was their anniversary, so he'd booked an inn in Niagara-on-the-Lake for one night with a wine tour. The extra time would allow him to plan some activities with his kids and some quality one-on-one time with his wife. She'd already planned for her parents to spend the night at their place to watch the kids. Knowing gramma and gramps would spoil them, they didn't complain too much that one of his nights at home would be away.

It annoyed Ryan that he had to fight with his dispatcher to get time off. But he didn't back down. They ran him hard, knowing he could handle whatever they threw at him, so he was a valuable employee. His marriage was more important to him than his job. He had well over 2 million accident-free miles under his belt. He could get work almost anywhere. Right now, the company needed him more than he needed them. His excellent driving record was a positive for the company's annual report.

After checking that, he put everything into his vehicle; he put it in gear and headed back to his house in Fergus, Ontario. It was a Thursday, so when he arrived home, the kids would still be in school, giving him some time to greet his wife without his children groaning.

He smiled at the thought. If he didn't hit traffic, there might even be time for something more. A sly grin played on his lips. His wife had kept her figure after having the kids. It helped that she ran five miles a day and did an hour of yoga. Knowing he was heading home, she often put on something sexy under her clothes as a surprise for him. Ryan knew that if she was feeling playful, she'd wear a dress and stockings. Fourteen years of marriage and the spark between them was as strong as ever.

He stopped at a Metro grocery store and picked up a ten-day flower bouquet, an anniversary card, and a bottle of wine on his way home. Better to come home bearing gifts than empty-handed on an anniversary weekend. She always told him she didn't want flowers when she was dead. Krissy wanted to enjoy them while she was alive. She also never asked for anything, which made making these simple gestures pleasurable.

Purchases in hand, he rushed back to his car. He'd make it home with time to spare. Ryan smiled when he turned off into his subdivision. The house was small but cozy, and Krissy kept it immaculate.

He pulled into his laneway and parked, leaving his gear behind. He grabbed the gifts and headed inside. Calling out, *'Wilma. I'm home.'* A private little joke between the two of them.

The house seemed eerily silent. He kicked off his shoes and went in search of Krissy. She popped out of the bathroom with a fresh coat of lipstick, just begging to be smudged, stockings, heels, and nothing else. He pulled her into a deep embrace, crushing her lips to his, the cold bottle of wine brushing against her buttocks.

"Welcome home, baby," Krissy whispered into his chest when he released her. He placed the bottle, flowers, and card on the sofa. Then scooped her up and carried her to their bedroom, his need for her straining against his jeans.

SATED AND DRESSED, Ryan poured them each a glass of wine while Krissy put the flowers in some water before the kids returned from school. He walked into the kitchen carrying both drinks and placed them on the counter. Then he went up to Krissy from behind, lifted her hair, and trailed light kisses on the base of her neck, up into her hairline. She shivered, causing him to smile as he let her hair drop back in place.

"Mr. Walker, don't you start anything you can't finish," she admonished.

"My dear Mrs. Walker, I believe I have already satisfied your carnal needs." He winked, handing her a wineglass.

"I hope you don't mind, but I thought we could order pizza tonight. That way, when the kids finish their homework, we can all play some games. Jessica is fond of Clue right now."

"That sounds perfect."

14

FRANK

Frank cursed under his breath; his tolerance level pushed to the breaking point. His dispatcher had forced him to take time off, which angered him. He hated not being on the road. It meant he'd have to spend time in his apartment in the city, one of his least favourite things to do. He felt more cooped up there than in his rig. He resented getting out of the truck. To him, his Mack was his home. He preferred to do his resets on the road, but the truck and trailer were both due for their annual safety inspection, and he didn't have a choice. It was a real pain in the ass. He had to remove his belongings from his truck; things he didn't want anyone else to see or touch. You didn't know whether the mechanic working on it was nosey and snooped or not.

Frank went through the truck and was careful to remove all of his stuff, not just his personal items, but his snacks as well. Some things he could leave behind, but others he couldn't. It was his truck, so he kept whatever he wanted in there and it should remain private, but he couldn't count on it. The mechanics needed his keys and would have full access to his cab.

The trailer was company-owned, and he didn't store belongings in there. They decided where and when to have the safety done. It

65

made sense for him to have his truck done there too and get the company discount. He didn't want to waste any more time than necessary sitting at home, so it just made sense. Frank didn't care that much about his personal things. It was his souvenirs that he valued and protected. The long ribbon with his mementos clipped to it. It was something he kept hanging within reach as he drove. Yes, he'd be sure to take everything out of the truck before he went home.

He shoved his clothing and snacks into his duffle bag after placing his souvenirs in the front pocket for safekeeping and tossed it onto the passenger seat of his rusty old Range Rover. He inserted the key into the ignition, prayed it would start after sitting for so long, and turned it. It clicked and chugged, but didn't catch. Frank cursed out loud and slammed his fist onto the dashboard before trying again. After a few false starts, the engine caught. Satisfied, he lit his third cigarette since climbing in before noticing that the tank was almost empty. He'd need to fill up before he went home. Frank cursed again. He knew he should have filled it before he parked it; but he'd hurried back to his rig, eager to get back on the road. Frank didn't worry about the fuel level of his pickup when he parked it. He pulled out of the yard and hit the first gas station he came to. He debated on only putting in twenty bucks, but figured he'd better fill it. If he didn't use it all, he'd still have gas in the tank when he got back. That way if he had to take time off again, he'd still have gas, plus he didn't know how long he'd be home for and might need a full tank.

It was a half hour's drive back to his apartment. His flat wasn't much, but it was cheap and he wasn't home often, anyway. He resented having to waste good money for a place he only used a few times a year. It would be cheaper to rent a motel as he needed it than to pay rent, but he didn't have a choice.

He pulled into the parking lot of his building and swore a long stream of expletives when he realized that someone had parked in his spot. It wasn't the first time either. He was pretty sure who it was; and was 100% sure the Super gave the old bat permission to park there. He slid his truck behind the bitch's vehicle and blocked her in. If he wasn't worried about being towed, he'd leave it like that.

Knowing his luck, someone would call parking control on him, and it would cost him a pretty penny to get it back. No, he'd better find the superintendent. She could find the old biddy to move the car. Frank stormed off towards the building. As soon as he stepped through the front door, he found the Super in the lobby, mopping the floor.

"Hey! Some fucking asshole is in my spot!"

THE SUPER WAS weary when she looked up at him. Wracking her brain, trying to remember which of her tenants he was. Then she realized, Carter, Frank Carter, trucker, apartment 103. Crap, he was home. She took a step back and shuddered. There was something about him that made her flesh crawl. He was an ass, true, but something else was lurking just beneath the surface that she couldn't put her finger on.

"I'm sorry about that, Mr. Carter. Let me check which car it is and get it moved. In the meantime, why don't you park in visitors?"

"Get the fuckwad towed. That's my spot, and I pay for it." As he spoke, he stepped closer to her. His face reddened with rage.

"Yes, I realized that. I'm sure it's just a misunderstanding."

She knew darn well who parked there. This jackass just got home, and his spot was the closest to the building. She'd allowed Mrs. Travers to use it when he wasn't here. The poor woman needed a walker. She qualified for a handicapped spot, but there wasn't enough available. The building was full of aging tenants. She had tried to get the spot transferred to Mrs. Travers, even asking this buffoon to switch places, but he'd refused. There was no way she'd call a towing company. She'd go up to Mrs. Travers herself, get her key and move it. She didn't want him to see whose car it was, or he'd cause more trouble. He may suspect who it belonged to, but he couldn't be sure. If she asked Mrs. Travers to move it, he'd spew a slew of insults her way. The woman was too fragile. The Super's mind raced for a solution. Then she found the answer.

"I'll tell you what. Why don't you let me give your place a quick clean for your trouble of having to park in visitors? I know you don't get home often, and I'm betting it's the last thing you want to do is clean your home. You can let me know if that works for you."

She watched as he eyed her up and down.

FRANK MULLED IT OVER. Getting the place cleaned was a good idea. He always left it a mess; he couldn't remember the last time he'd cleaned it. Frank chuckled to himself. This situation worked out in his favour. He'd let the Super in to clean. If she did it now, it would be ready for him. His duffle bag was still in his vehicle and there was nothing personal in his apartment, so he wasn't worried.

"Ok. I'll let you clean my place. Now's a good time. You can clean it while I grab a burger. That car had better be gone when I return! If not, I'll report you and the owner of the car to management."

He turned and stomped off.

THE SUPER BREATHED a sigh of relief when he was out of sight. Then she raced up to get Mrs. Travers' key and move the car back to the correct spot. She'd have to work fast to get his apartment cleaned. She didn't know how long he'd be. Or what kind of mess she'd be facing when she got there.

After moving Mrs. Travers' car, she went to apartment 103 and let herself in. As soon as she entered, the odour of rotting food, stale smoke, filth, and dust assaulted her senses. She ran to the window, pulled up the blinds, and opened it to let in some fresh air. She paused when she saw the pair of binoculars, thick with dust on the window ledge.

Letting the image sit in the back of her mind, she proceeded to the kitchen. The trash was overflowing in the bin. A mass on the floor was crawling with maggots. Her stomach heaved twice before she realized she couldn't stop it, and she vomited in the kitchen sink. She turned on the water to wash it away and splashed her face.

This place was disgusting. Now she was glad she'd had the fore-thought to bring rubber gloves. Who knew what else she'd find? Old takeout cartons littered the counter. Mold seeped through the cracks and out onto the countertop. She pulled out a large green garbage bag and began throwing out the old cartons of takeout and the over-flowing basket of trash. She used an old dustpan to scoop up the maggot covered, whatever it was, and tossed that too. When she opened the fridge, she found more of the same green, slimy, rotted food. The only thing clean was the stove. It was apparent Mr. Carter had never used it. It only needed a quick wipe to remove the dust.

Right away she regretted her offer to clean, but filled a bucket anyway and got to work. When she finished the kitchen, she cleaned the central area and washed the floor. She wouldn't open the Murphy bed. Whatever was in there was his issue.

Next, she tackled the washroom. Grime and whiskers stuck to the sink, toilet, and tub. Here she needed a scrub brush to cut through the stuck-on sludge. Once cleaned, she finished up by grab-bing the garbage in the kitchen. She was thankful now that she'd made the offer. The longer he lived here, the worse it would get. God knows what she'd have found when he moved out if she hadn't cleaned his place today.

She was relieved to find the place wasn't full of cockroaches. That would have been too much for her to handle. It would have meant an infestation in the entire building. The maintenance budget couldn't cover an exterminator right now.

She surveyed the apartment and considered it a job well done. Then she remembered the binoculars. She grabbed her dust cloth to dust them and the windowsill off. Now that she had them in her hand, she looked to see what it was Carter looked at. He wasn't a birdwatcher; of that, she was certain. She looked around, but from this angle, the only thing she had a good view of was the school. She flinched as the realization that he watched the children washed over her. In her haste to leave, she dropped the binoculars on the ledge, hoping she didn't crack the lens.

She couldn't get out of the apartment fast enough. Only stopping to grab the garbage and her cleaning supplies as she left. Her stomach heaved, and she felt the sudden need to wash the filth from her body. Just being in that apartment made her feel dirty, but the thought that he spied on the children when he was home repulsed her. When she was clean, she'd take the car keys back to Mrs. Travers.

WHEN HE RETURNED, Frank walked into his apartment and dropped his bag on the floor. He looked around and chuckled to himself. He felt he'd pulled one over on the Super. True, it pissed him off that someone was in his spot. But as soon as she offered to clean his apartment, he knew he'd say yes. He hadn't been home in months and couldn't even remember if he'd taken out the garbage.

He sniffed the air and thought he could make out the aroma of rotten food amongst the odour of cleaning solution. Yup, he thought, he'd forgotten to take out the trash. He'd have to remember to do it this time. It was unlikely he'd con the Super into cleaning his place again. Somehow, things always worked out in his favour. This apartment, for instance, was located close to his yard. There were fast-food places nearby, and it was on the first floor. There was even a school across the street. When he was home, he could sit in his window and watch the kids play or walk to and from school. Even though he'd be happier to stay in his truck, being here wasn't a poor alternative.

Now that his apartment was clean, and he didn't have to deal with whatever he'd left on the counter, he could relax. He'd do his laundry and shower. He sniffed under his arm; yup, he needed a shower first. He checked his watch. If he hurried, he could watch the kids get out of school. As he showered, he wondered if there were any new students.

15

NAPANEE, ONTARIO

$\mathcal{I}$n the driver's lounge of the truck stop, a pair of watchful eyes scanned the surroundings, missing nothing. Forgotten on the ground was a shower bag kicked to one side, the slip of paper with the shower entry code crumpled tight within a fist. Nearby, a little girl played alone, too far from her unobservant parents, too engrossed in their respective phones. Another pair of eyes belonging to a lone man, locked onto the little girl as she moved further from her parents and closer to his hiding place.

The first person remained hidden from view of the would-be assailant, waiting to make a move, but only if necessary. Praying the parents would look up and notice their child had moved beyond their sight, but also knowing the man whose eyes hadn't left the child was another sick, twisted, subhuman who needed to die. The area was too public. Taking care of predators was best done in the dark of night, or in secluded locales. But if the man grabbed the child, an intervention would happen, no matter the consequences.

The observer kicked the shower bag on the floor. One foot shoved it against the door to shower number three. The code on the tiny piece of paper memorized and stuffed into a pocket, pulling out a small pocketknife at the same time flipping it open to be ready. It was not the preferred weapon, but one of necessity.

The depraved man watching the child glanced around as she came within reach. His meaty hand darted out, clamping over the child's small cherub mouth before she could utter a sound as he pulled her to him. An unlocked utility closet was nearby, and he carried her there. His hand clamped across her mouth. Her tiny feet kicked in the air. He stepped back into the closet before turning to ensure they were alone. A foot shot out, preventing the door from closing behind the attacker. The man held the child in his arms, unaware of the person behind him. The hand with the open pocket knife grasped within in a fist, pressed against his jugular.

"Let her go," a voice hissed in his ear.

He tried to turn, but the knife dug in deeper. Not having a choice, he released his grasp on the child, and she tumbled to the ground. The child scrambled to her feet; her eyes were wide with fear as she stared at the man who had taken her. The child's rescuer hidden from view.

"Run!" the voice urged with a hiss.

The child rushed past them, pausing as she fumbled with the doorknob before she opened the door enough for her to escape. As she ran, the knife plunged deep into the man's neck. Blood squirted in pulses as he fell into the wash bucket, spilling the dirty water on the floor to mingle with the pooling blood. There wasn't time for the barrette. It didn't matter, anyway; the killer was unprepared. To hide the crime, the killer stuffed the bloodied hands and knife into coat pockets. The door cracked open to check for witnesses before the killer jogged to shower three. Using a clean finger to press the memorized code onto the keypad, the door opened and a foot kicked the shower bag inside. The door locked, and the killer breathed a deep sigh. Soon, the child would be in the safety of her parents' arms, and the angry father or the police would discover the body.

With a twist of the tap, the shower started. The rushing water drowned out the commotion outside in the hall. An angry face looked into the mirror, flushed, ire and hate still emanating from rage-filled eyes. Washing the blood from the rain jacket would be easy.

Cleaning the knife in the shower would remove the traces of blood. There was no reason to hurry. Confident that the child saw no one but her potential abductor, the killer felt safe. Therefore, a nice, long shower would wash away all traces of blood, a squirt of bleach from the shower bag would help finish the job.

16

DETECTIVE COLBY TATE

*D*etective Tate sat at his desk pondering his case load. He drummed his fingers, feeling like they had benched him when his superior dropped the most recent stack of files on him to review. One case he'd been working on just went to trial, so his load had lightened. In front of him were the case files of six murder victims. They found the bodies in different provinces, but all were at truck stops along the Trans-Canada Highway. Each of the victims had died of exsanguination from a knife wound to the neck. A single piece of evidence tied all the cases together except the last one his boss threw in because the victimology was the same. Although the killer used a knife; it wasn't the same MO, and the kill was sloppy. So far, the others had been clean, with a single slice across the throat left to right, showing that the killer was right-handed. They'd found no evidence at the crime scenes to indicate the identity of the killer. The only consistent piece of evidence was the child's hair clip. He wasn't sure the other case belonged with the rest. The key piece of evidence missing from that case was the hair clip.

All the victims so far were truck drivers, and all the locations were at truck stops. The seventh case was a truck driver and happened at a truck stop, but the trinket was missing. They almost

74

overlooked it with the first victim, but they were fortunate the local police did their job and gathered everything they'd found at the crime scene. It was the same trinket left near all the bodies, except one, a child's small, pink plastic hair barrette.

They couldn't find a connection except all the victims were truck drivers. Nothing else linked the cases together other than the barrette and method of killing. All the locations were different and spread across the country. He pulled up the report on the man at the Flying J, and spread the crime scene photos out on the desk in front of him. This kill was more violent. Yes, the weapon used was a knife, but it was smaller, a pocket knife, according to the report. The erratic, repeated stab wounds appeared personal and more aggressive, whereas the others were clean and with skill. One smooth slice across the throat. The cut on the first victim's throat almost decapitated him. He was about to toss what he considered being an unrelated file aside, dismissing it as not belonging with the rest, when he noticed another report clipped to the back of it.

He flipped it over and began reading. The dead man had grabbed a child and pulled her into a storage closet. Someone rescued the girl, and when they went in search of the abductor a short while later, they discovered the man dead. The description the child gave of her assailant matched that of the victim. Tate understood the girl was lucky to have escaped. Someone intervened and told her to run. By the time the police arrived, they'd found the body and a gathering crowd, but the killer was long gone. The child remembered nothing about her rescuer. Maybe the common denominator was little girls. The barrettes belonged to young girls. The child, almost abducted, was a young girl. Could this be a vigilante? Colby pulled out his note pad and began making notes regarding his theory.

The crimes spread from coast to coast, all at truck stops off of the Trans-Canada Highway. It surprised him they'd linked the cases together so soon. But maybe it wasn't as soon as he thought. Colby hit the search button on his computer and entered a few more details and waited.

"Holy Shit!" he exclaimed as several more hits popped up.

When it finished, it identified at least a half dozen more victims, all spanning the last five years. How had they missed this? He sent a request for the rest of the files to be sent over. It was time to set up a command post. They had a serial killer on the loose.

He grabbed his notes and went to speak to his supervisor. They needed to get a profile on the killer and re-investigate the past cases. His supervisor agreed and sent him off to work his way across Canada to investigate the crimes as the act of a serial killer. He needed to speak with witnesses, police officers, and coroners. The wounds would give them certain information, such as what they already knew, which was that the killer was right-handed. But the wounds should reveal how tall the killer was as well. The bodies would tell a story, they always did.

One thing he knew for sure, their killer had been very busy.

17

MAGGIE

*M*aggie was busy engrossed in her phone as she entered the washroom and didn't see the woman exiting before she bumped into her. Without looking up, she mumbled, 'sorry,' then she raised her head and made eye contact. Her eyes widened when she recognized Noelle, the lot-lizard from Chilliwack.

'What is she doing here?' Maggie wondered.

Noelle's step faltered as she realized who she bumped into. Maggie knew by Noelle's expression that she didn't expect to run into anyone she knew out in Enfield, Nova Scotia. She saw Noelle hesitate and almost speak to her, but she lowered her head and left.

Even though Maggie noticed Noelle pause, she dismissed it. Instead, she concentrated on what Noelle was doing so far from home. She looked back at Noelle's retreating figure. Then it occurred to her. Noelle had hitched a ride with a trucker and travelled east. Whatever happened, it wasn't her concern. She knew Noelle could take care of herself.

WHEN MAGGIE FINISHED in the washroom, she stopped by the convenience store to grab a couple of Red Bulls and a pack of smokes before she headed back to her rig. She wasn't in a hurry, so she took the long way around as she walked through the parking lot. In the distance, she glimpsed Noelle climb up into an Erb truck parked in the rear row. She sighed to herself and wondered what happened that led Noelle to choose that profession. There were other things she could do to earn a living. She knew that for some; it was drugs, but from what she could see, Noelle was clean. It made little sense to her.

Maggie tossed the Red Bulls up into the cab, pulled a cigarette out of the package, and lit it. Then she walked to the rear of her rig, unlocked the trailer door, and looked inside to check her load. Everything was fine. The straps on the wheels were tight. She'd only just loaded in the port, but it never hurt to double-check. She'd run out of hours and would spend the night here before hitting the road again early in the morning. Maggie swung the trailer door closed and secured the lock, ground out her smoke, before she climbed back up into the cab. Time to figure out what she was having for dinner. She'd shower after she ate, then settle in for the night.

AFTER HER SHOWER, Maggie stepped out into the cool summer night air and realized she didn't feel like heading straight back to the truck. She looked around the lot, scanning along the rows of trucks, hoping to see someone she recognized. Maggie was quick to realize there was no one she knew. So, she resigned herself to a quiet night. She'd head back to her rig, throw on a movie and climb up on her bunk.

She hung her towel up to dry; thumbed through her collection of DVDs before selecting one. She pulled down the TV and placed it on the table, then plugged it in and inserted the movie. It was too early to get undressed, but she'd set up her pee bucket just in case. She'd fashioned a five-gallon bucket with a kitchen catcher, some kitty litter, and a pool noodle into a makeshift toilet. It was handy if she had to pee at night. The act of getting dressed and making her way into the truck stop brought her wide awake. It was worse in the winter. After leaving the truck to use the washroom, she never got back to sleep. So having the bucket available prevented that. A quick pee and back to bed. In the morning, she'd toss the bag. Easy-peasy!

She fluffed up her pillows and unbuttoned her jeans before she leaned back to watch the movie. It was a thriller from a multipack she'd picked up out of the $5 bin at Walmart. She grabbed a bottle of water, knowing the Red Bull would keep her awake, and pulled down a bag of chips. She wanted a cold beer, but that could wait until Cobden, when she visited with her dad and went to see her Aunt Julie.

Her route back would take her right through town. This time she'd stop and see her aunt, or it would create drama for herself. She loved her aunt and uncle, but they worried too much. What she should do was give her aunt a heads up and let her know she was coming. She was due for an oil change, and she could kill two birds with one stone.

She checked her phone. It was still early enough to call Aunt Julie. She paused the movie and dialled her aunt.

"Hello?" Her aunt's voice was soft, a far cry from the woman who could make a grown man wither with a single look.

"Hey, Aunt Julie."

"Maggie?"

"Yes, it's me."

"Is everything ok?"

Maggie heard the concern in her aunt's voice. It had been too long between calls if Julie thought something was wrong.

"Oh, ya, everything's good. I'll be in Cobden the day after tomorrow. I plan to visit dad and thought I'd visit you as well."

"It's about time!" Julie exclaimed.

Maggie rolled her eyes before responding. She expected this reaction.

"Well, you're not exactly off the highway like dad is." She nibbled her lip, now regretting her decision to book an oil change at the same time.

Julie sighed, then asked, "What time will you be here?"

"I should be there early afternoon." Maggie responded.

"Your Uncle will be home for his reset tomorrow. Will you stay for dinner?"

"Uh, um, sure."

"Good, and yes, bring the truck in for an oil change."

Maggie sputtered. "H... h... how did you know?"

Julie just laughed. "Maggie, I helped raise you. Did you think I wouldn't hear the hesitation in your voice? Or the guilt at the time between calls and visits? Dammit, girl, don't do that to yourself, but please try to stop in more often. If you can't come off the highway, let me know. I'd leave the shop and meet you when you see your dad."

"You're right Aunt Julie. I'll do better in the future."

Julie snorted. "At least try. I have to run, a late customer. See you in a couple of days. Love you, kiddo."

"Love you too."

She always felt guilty when she talked to her aunt. She didn't know why. Her aunt and uncle accepted who she was. They understood her need for solitude and the open road. They kidded with her but didn't add to her guilt even if she didn't visit very often. The feelings of guilt were her own doing. Aunt Julie never made a big deal about it. It didn't stop her aunt from busting her chops, though.

She'd attempt to do better. It was possible for her to stop in once every two months. She just didn't. Maggie adored her aunt and uncle, and she wouldn't be where she was now without them. It was just that she preferred to be alone. Her desire for seclusion was why she chose truck driving, like her father and her uncle before her, even with her excellent grades and options open to be anything she wanted. It was the perfect lifestyle for the independent person who enjoyed solitude.

She set her alarm, put the phone on to charge, and got out of her clothes. She'd use the bucket to pee in when she finished the movie. Maggie closed the curtains and locked the doors before climbing in under the covers. She needed to relax and not worry about her upcoming visit with her family. They loved and accepted her. She knew that even if they didn't know everything about her.

18

NOELLE

*N*oelle smiled to herself at the knowledge she was heading west. The Erb driver had given her a ride into Quebec, which was more than she'd hoped for. He pulled into the Irving truck stop at exit 145 off Highway 20, before heading to his depot to change trailers. The driver liked the idea of getting sex for free, for giving her a ride in the direction that he was already going. He made her stay on the bunk in the back. He couldn't allow anyone to see her, or he'd have hell to pay. It was against company policy to have riders in the cab. He also told her he didn't mind giving her a ride, as he could use the company. Life on the road was lonely.

He hadn't treated her as well as Mark had. He'd made her pay for her meals, but he only expected sex that once, so it wasn't too bad. Getting another ride from here would prove challenging. Quebec was full of French-speaking drivers. Even those who could speak English often pretended not to understand. She was a long way from home and the weather was getting colder. It was time to return. She wouldn't lower her standards, but she'd take a ride with whomever she could.

If she played her cards right, she might get lucky and find a single driver heading straight to Chilliwack. That was what she hoped for. The constant searching for a driver who would give her a ride was exhausting. She'd found there were fewer drivers wanting her company on the eastern side of Canada. They liked the sex; but they didn't want to give her a ride. It was always the same excuse, 'company policy.' You'd think company policy would include getting fucked in the back of your truck, but she wasn't one to argue when she was working.

As soon as he stopped the truck, she'd hopped out, gave him a quick thank you, and made her way to the building. She needed to pee and grab a hot coffee. She entered through the driver's lounge and looked around for a possible new companion. It was empty. Dammit, finding another ride may be more challenging than she thought. Things were different here. The cops were sneakier. She'd have to be cautious as she worked the lot. It was a good thing it was still early in the day. She could hang out in the lounge and try to find a ride that way.

She made her way to the woman's washroom. When she finished, she splashed some water on her face to refresh herself. Finding herself alone, she checked her wallet to see how much cash she still had. She counted out the bills, sticking a few in a different compartment of her bag for safekeeping. Satisfied she was ok and had plenty of money to get home, she went to the restaurant to order a hot meal. She'd take her time eating and then head to Tim Horton's for a coffee. After she'd go to the driver's lounge and hope to find someone heading west who'd like some company. If all else failed, she'd begin the tedious task of going truck to truck.

19

RYAN

*H*is romantic getaway with Krissy was what they both needed, a chance to reconnect and rekindle the passion they shared. Their relationship was fine, but trucking was hard on a marriage. They spent too many hours apart, missing the day-to-day things. If you wanted it to work, you had to try. Ryan took every opportunity to let Krissy know how much she meant to him, and Krissy reciprocated. It's what made their marriage work.

He hated saying goodbye to Krissy and the kids, but he had to. When he and Krissy returned from their quick getaway, they spent a couple of great days with the kids. They went on hikes, tossed the line in the water, played board games and watched a movie. Now the kids were back in school, Krissy was back in her own routine and he was back in his truck.

Ryan loaded his gear into his truck and made his bed, knowing that when he stopped, he'd be too tired to bother after thirteen hours of driving. He shook out his sheets, and a piece of paper fell to the floor. He bent over, picked it up, noting that Krissy's neat scrawl filled the page. *'Thanks for a great weekend. I love you. Krissy.'* A broad smile swept across his face. Yes, it was the little things.

After making his bed, he tucked the note in his visor before starting his log so he could head out and pick up his load. He checked his paperwork to verify where he was going and what he was picking up. Ryan entered his pickup location into his GPS and pulled out of the yard. He ran the route through his mind and realized it would be a couple of weeks before he'd make it back. He wished dispatch would give him a heads up when he was still at home instead of just leaving the paperwork in his locker. Krissy liked to know when she packed and prepared his food how much he'd need. Once again, he'd run out of meals before he returned home. He'd have to stop somewhere and pick up some frozen dinners at a grocery store along the way. They wouldn't be like Krissy's, but they'd fill the void. When he stopped at his pickup location, he'd send her a quick text letting her know the time frame.

HE PULLED into the lot to collect his load and, while he waited, fired off the text to Krissy. They used a crane to lift the cargo onto his flat deck, so until it was in place, there was nothing for him to do but wait. When it was on his trailer, that's when he had the responsibility of tarping and fastening the straps. That was one of the worst parts of flat decking. Sometimes he'd have to battle with the tarps when it was windy and raining. The deck could get slippery when it rained or snowed, but the per-mile pay was higher, which helped him to support his family. That was the reason Krissy could stay home with the kids. He looked at the temperature gauge on his dash and thought it would soon be time to add his winter gear to his truck and put away his shorts and tees. The weather was getting cooler and was unpredictable this time of year.

He wondered if he should bite the bullet and buy a truck of his own, but he'd heard too many horror stories about emission issues with sensors going every couple of months. Sensors could run almost two grand, then add a tow bill and hotels on top of the repair costs and it could cripple his family's finances. So, for now, he would continue as a company driver. The company could cover the cost of fuel and repairs.

He looked up at the darkening sky and knew there was rain coming, which meant he'd get soaked when he delivered. Krissy always said he was like a cat and hated getting wet. He chuckled at the thought. Sometimes the snow was better. It was just as slippery on the deck, but repelled better off his coat. Of course, his fingers got numb in the cold. He found it was difficult to get the straps tight enough when he wore gloves. Thank God for the heater inside the truck. Then rain or snow, it didn't matter. It would warm up his core.

His CB crackled with talk about another murdered driver. He wondered how long he could keep the news from Krissy. He knew she'd find out sooner or later. The last thing she needed was to worry about a crazy person who killed truck drivers.

20

FRANK

rank couldn't stand staying in one place for too long. Yes, he'd enjoyed watching the kids, but it wasn't the same. He didn't have the same opportunities so close to home. He sighed and stepped away from the window. They were in their classroom until recess, time to turn on the tube. As he settled onto his couch, his cell phone chirped. The display read 'Dispatch.'

'It's about time.' He thought.

"Hello."

"Hi Frank."

"Are my truck and trailer ready?"

"Yup, that's why I'm calling. We've got a load for you to North Carolina. Can you get here within two hours?"

"That won't be a problem. Is my truck in the yard? Or do I have to get it?"

"No, don't worry, it's back in the yard. The mechanics dropped it off a few minutes ago."

"Perfect, I'll see you soon." He said before ending the call.

Frank only needed to throw a few items into his duffel bag. Most of what he'd washed, he'd already put back in his bag. Then he reached under his pillow and pulled out his ribbon of souvenirs, and stuffed it in the front pocket of his pack and zipped it closed for safe keeping. He grabbed the pop and chips he was about to open; no need to leave these behind. The trash bag was overflowing, so he'd toss it on his way out of the building. If he wasn't careful, his place would be full of roaches, and they'd send in an exterminator when he wasn't home. He didn't like the thought of people snooping through his stuff. Frank lowered the blinds and closed the curtains to keep out prying eyes. He looked at the school one last time. It was unfortunate he missed the recess break, but he'd been home long enough. With his bag and garbage collected, he left and locked the door.

He tossed the trash in the bin outside the back door and walked the few steps to his truck before tossing his duffle on the passenger seat. Frank started his vehicle, looked at his gas gauge, and was thankful he'd filled up when he first got home. He was eager to get back on the open road and search for a new memento to add to his collection.

21

CALGARY, ALBERTA

ingers pulled the last of the pink hair barrettes from the
package and placed it in the front pocket of faded, well-
worn denim jeans. There were faint splatters of dried blood that
speckled the pale, tattered fabric near the booted feet. The next
victim was in sight. Nearby vigilant eyes watched the man leave the
casino; his body swayed as he stumbled back to his rig. He'd had one
too many beers as he gambled his pay cheque away.

The constant truck traffic kept the parking lot too busy for the
knife to find its mark. No, not yet. It was best to practice patience as
the other drivers ended their night and headed back to retire. The
rain poncho and veterinary gloves remained hidden in a pocket, so
they'd be ready as soon as the opportunity presented itself. Inside the
jacket, a unique sheath housed the latest knife, keeping it out of
sight. The blade of choice was ceramic. Its sharpness made cutting
through flesh as easy as slicing butter. The bonus was that ceramic
knives were easy to come by and untraceable. The only drawback
was that they sometimes broke, which meant having to replace them.

Boots hit the pavement with a dull thud as the killer jumped to
the ground from the cab of the rig. The impact softened with bent
knees. Now standing, the need to maintain the blood flowing in

muscles that stayed too long in one position prevailed as the assailant moved forward. Wisps of breath blew into the cool midnight air. The movement also helped keep warmth in the body. The perpetrator continued to move around the parking lot's perimeter, keeping to the shadows to avoid detection. It would be a long night. The right moment would present itself. The target drank to excess in the casino. Soon he'd have to pee. The killer hoped he'd step out of his truck and not use a bottle. The man wouldn't go back to the building to use the washroom. That was too far. Instead, he'd either stand in his doorway to pee or step out between the two trucks and use the cover of darkness to hide what he was doing.

The parking lot already reeked of stale urine from drivers who were too lazy to go inside. If he used the doorway, it would be problematic. The driver would react to a rain caped, gloved figure with a knife. It was possible to kill him on his steps, but too risky. At around 2:30 a.m., the cab lit up as the driver's door opened, and he stepped down between the trucks. The opportunity arose. Quick, silent steps brought the killer right behind the truck driver. The shadows hid the attacker, and another pervert would die with his dick in his hands. It was poetic justice. The knife slashed against the soft skin of the driver's throat, splitting it wide. Garbled words sprang from the victim's lips. He turned, hands at his throat as he tried to stop the bleeding, his pants unzipped, and his penis dangled as he faced his assailant. The cut wasn't deep enough for immediate death, but he'd still die from the blood loss. This time, it would take longer. Clean, quick kills were better, with less chance of being discovered. The driver's eyes widened in shock when he saw his attacker.

Once again, he tried to speak as blood seeped through his fingers before he collapsed on the pavement.

The assailant wiped blood from the knife, using the victim's shirt, then returned it to the sheath. The killer removed the blood-splattered poncho and gloves, balled them up, and placed them in a plastic garbage bag. On the ground beside the corpse, the tiny pink barrette dropped to the pavement, with the world rid of another deviant. Then the killer slipped away into the shadows.

22

DR. AUDREY COLEMAN

*D*r. Coleman glanced at her watch, noting that it was only mid-afternoon. She sighed when she realized that the day was dragging on. She still had another trial to testify at this afternoon before she finished her day. Today she'd spent most of the day testifying in court as an expert witness. She was a clinical psychiatrist, who specialized in children and childhood traumas. Absently, she fingered the fine leather band of her watch while she waited. Having it around her wrist comforted her. She knew very few people still wore a watch, preferring to use their cell phones to tell time. But she was from a different era and it was a gift from her husband.

THE JUDGE DISMISSED her after her testimony, and she was ready to head home. She slipped behind the wheel of her car and thought about the gin and tonic waiting for her, and she needed it. Court cases took a lot out of her. She felt drained, and after glancing in the rear-view mirror, she noticed the dark circles under her eyes, which confirmed it.

Audrey lived in a small cottage on a large lakefront property with her two cats, Ash and Blue, both seal point Siamese. She had a husband and child once. But they were both gone now, and she chose solitude.

She realized she should retire. But who would take over her practice? She continued counselling those that remained because she loved the one-on-one, her clients needed her and she no longer took on new clients. Audrey didn't see as many patients as she once did. At her age, she vowed not to add to her caseload. It wasn't fair not knowing how long she'd have to devote to working with them. Every past client she had still continued to reach out to her, to seek a counselling session from time to time, or to let her know how they were doing. One of her past clients concerned her.

She had counselled this one for almost ten years before the client ended the regular sessions. At the clients' insistence, she only referred to the case number when they spoke, case number 156. They still spoke from time to time. 156 called at regular intervals, no longer for counselling, their relationship had grown into an almost friendship. But she was worried.

Case 156 alluded to hints that the dark side had returned. The anger that lurked just below the surface had bubbled up. She couldn't get 156 to elaborate, at least not yet. Audrey hoped 156 would open up and soon. It was the only way she could offer assistance.

She just hoped things weren't as bad as she suspected. She'd heard the news stories about truck drivers being killed along The Trans-Canada Highway. The murders caused her to worry about two things: one, if 156 was involved, and two, was 156 safe? She'd have to tread with caution during the next call to get the answers she wanted.

23

DETECTIVE COLBY TATE

*D*etective Tate parked the car he'd rented when he arrived in Sudbury. He was now at the Petro Pass where they'd discovered the first victim. He'd studied and ran a search through the database and found other cases with victims killed using the same methodology, and concluded that this was the initial kill site. The first thing he noticed was that the location wasn't large, but seemed to fit all the requirements a trucker needed, washrooms, showers, and snacks. The truck stop was just off the Trans-Canada Highway, which was another factor. Because the killer seemed to avoid detection, Colby wondered if another trucker was the killer.

He stepped out of his car and wandered around the lot. He realized he wouldn't find any trace evidence after all these years. The murder happened just over five years ago. But he wanted to get a feel for the place and check things out. 'How could a murder go unnoticed?' He wondered. 'Why here? Was it a matter of opportunity?' He looked around at the open fields that surrounded the area; he couldn't believe no one saw anything.

As he walked behind a row of parked trucks, he realized it was because of this; the crime went undetected. At night, the rigs blocked the view of the pumps. All the murders happened at night when there was less traffic, except the one in Napanee, but he still wasn't sure if it connected to the rest.

Colby made his way inside the building to talk with the workers. He introduced himself to the manager, who told him that a complete changeover in the staff had taken place since the murder. He heaved a deep sigh. Colby had their names and contact information, but it would be more time-consuming tracking them down. He made his way back to his car and flipped through the file. He was due to meet with the investigating police officer at the local police department in half an hour. Colby wandered around and took a few pictures before he left.

He had a few minutes to spare, so he took out his pen and began making a list of queries he had for the officer. Plus, he wanted access to the evidence gathered at the crime scene. He pulled out the crime scene photographs and wondered how much rage someone needed to inflict the wounds on the victim's neck. Was the killer a powerful person? Did the wound require strength or a very sharp knife? Or both? His mind rolled with questions and possibilities.

Forensics couldn't determine the type of knife, other than it had a smooth sharp blade at least seven inches long. Detective Tate flipped through the file. There weren't a lot of notes attached to the photos. The only witnesses were after the fact. Someone discovered the body the following day. No one saw or heard anything. In truck stops, there was too much transient traffic. Trucks passed through all day and night. Their killer could be anyone.

It appeared they had an experienced sociopath on their hands. Someone who understood how the trucking industry worked and the routines of the drivers. They were looking for someone who frequented truck stops or drove a truck. Tate made a couple more notes on his theories and thoughts before closing the file and heading to the station.

24

THE KILLER

The killer leaned back, holding the empty container that housed the tools of the trade and realized that it was time to go shopping. The dwindling supplies necessary to complete the kills needed to be replaced. Only one complete set remained. The hunt continued for one man in particular; the man who started it all. Would killing that one particular man put an end to the rage that led to all of this violence? The killer hoped so. Anything to stop the uncontrollable anger that bubbled up from within. How many more needed to die before the right one met his end? There was a sense of satisfaction knowing that the victims deserved their deaths. They were all perverted bastards who preyed on children. The sense of contentment radiated with each kill, but it was still somewhat hollow. The real satisfaction would be to put an end to that one man. Each death became an opportunity to rid the world of vile scum. Nothing more, nothing less. There was no guilt. So far, the RCMP hadn't connected the crimes together; these deviants who always lurked in the shadows. With every kill, it seemed another took his place; a never-ending barrage of sickos.

Replacing the barrettes and rain ponchos was a simple task. Most dollar stores carried them. Because dollar stores were often in strip malls, there was enough parking for a truck. The elbow-length veterinary gloves were a different matter. They had to be sourced from a farm supply store. It wasn't always easy to park a truck and trailer nearby, but there were a few close enough to other retail places with parking. Purchasing the gloves online would be easier, but it would leave a record. Any purchases made had to be paid for with cash. Using cash avoided a paper trail.

There was an advantage in travelling coast to coast across Canada. Most people working in stores didn't recognize you if you hadn't visited for several months, plus there was the probability of staff turnover. When you stopped in, you had to be friendly. But not overly. It was also important to wear nondescript clothing and not call attention to yourself. That's how you remained unmemorable. Nothing could stand out for a cashier to remember. It was easier to be unremarkable than most people thought. Most criminals got caught because they weren't smart. They got cocky and made mistakes. Being smart was a necessity when seeking redemption; as was being careful.

25

MAGGIE

*M*aggie called her dispatcher and explained that she planned to take a few days off before she returned to the yard. She knew there wouldn't be a problem because her load didn't have a specific delivery time. She needed an oil change and to visit with her aunt and uncle, as she promised. Her aunt's compound was secure, so the trailer and the cars inside would remain safe. Adam told her not to worry and enjoy her family time. He knew she didn't ask for time off very often and deserved the break.

Then she called her aunt back to confirm she was coming. She didn't give her an exact time, so she pulled off to have a quick visit with her dad before heading to the shop. Maggie parked at the side of the road and put on her four ways. She did a quick jog up the hill to spend a half-hour with her dad in the warm sunshine before continuing to her aunt's shop.

The shop wasn't far. Julie's shop was only a few kilometres away, and her house was next door. It gave Uncle Bobbie a place to park his truck when he was home, too. Maggie had spent a lot of time both in the shop and house when she was growing up. Her Aunt taught her about mechanics, which proved invaluable when she bought her rig. It saved her a fortune being able to do quick repairs on the road herself.

After visiting with her dad, she continued on to the shop. She saw the sign for Hopkins Repairs as it loomed ahead, then she turned into the lot and parked out front. There was a whoosh of air as she pulled the brake and the truck settled. First, she'd greet her aunt and find out when she wanted the cab pulled inside for the oil change. Maggie turned off the ignition and climbed out. As soon as her boots hit the gravel, she felt at home. She'd grown up in and around the shop. She could pull her truck into the shop and change the oil herself, but her aunt wouldn't hear of it. Julie wouldn't want Maggie working on her truck when she had a group of mechanics to do it for her.

In her storage compartment, she carried a small tool kit, and as long as it wasn't electronic, she could fix it herself. She used a small area of the trailer to keep spare parts and lights. Doing her own repairs meant getting back on the road sooner, especially if it was something as simple as a burned-out light.

She scanned the yard and noticed her uncle's truck in the back. She smiled, seeing his rig. It was perfect. Now they'd have dinner together, she'd spend the night and be able to get back on the road sooner than she'd expected.

"Maggie, girl!" Uncle Bobbie's voice boomed from the house.

Maggie swung around with a grin stretched across her face as she waved in greeting. She almost ran over to hug him, but before she could, she heard her aunt call out.

"Hey, sweetie." Aunt Julie stepped out of the shop, her hair tied back in a messy ponytail, oil-stained coveralls, and she was wiping her hands off on a rag.

Maggie went to her aunt, kissed her on the cheek, and stepped back before Julie wrapped her arms around her in a bear hug. Maggie didn't want grease on her clothes.

"Hi, Aunt Julie. It's good to see you. Did you want me to park the trailer and pull my truck into the bay?"

"Yup, I kept bay one empty for you. My day's almost done. I'll have one of the boys give her the once over first thing in the morning. He'll get it all lubed up and ready for you." Julie rocked back on her heels as she observed Maggie.

"Did you want me to wait for you before heading to the house?"

"Are you kidding? Bobbie would tear a strip off me if I held you up any longer than necessary. He's dying to find out what you've been hauling. Besides that, he misses you. We both do."

Maggie ran her fingers through her hair and looked sideways at her aunt.

"I'll try to come home more often."

Julie laughed. "Don't make promises you can't keep. I realize you have to go where the loads take you, but you can call. We worry and want to know you're ok."

Maggie felt her cheeks burn. She looked down, then gave her aunt a sly glimpse before responding.

"Ok, deal. Let me move the truck and grab my overnight bag. Did you need me to start supper?"

"No. You know your uncle; he's been up there cooking up a storm. He'll say you're too skinny and need to eat more."

Maggie looked down at her tiny frame and sighed. With the enclosed car division, being slim was an asset. Stout drivers couldn't climb in and out of the car windows inside the trailer. There was limited space, but she slid in and out with ease. She realized her uncle would pack a 'doggy bag' of food for her when she left, which she'd accept willingly.

Before she could comment on her size being an asset in her line of work, a pair of arms grabbed her from behind and swung her in the air. When her feet were back on the ground, she turned and allowed her uncle to pull her in for a bear hug. It comforted her to breathe in the familiar scent of his cologne mixed with the liniment he rubbed into his joints.

"Oh, Maggie girl, I've missed you. Let me have a look at you." Bobbie said as he stepped back. He kept his hands on her shoulders as he looked her over.

Noticing the cigarette tucked behind her ear, he reached out and snatched it away, brought it to his lips, and lit it. He looked over Maggie's shoulder at his wife. "Your Aunt is trying to get me to quit.

When I'm home, she rations them out." He chuckled with a deep, hardy laugh.

Julie just shook her head, causing Maggie to laugh. There was no way her aunt could control how much he smoked on the road, but she knew Julie kept a tight rein on him at home.

"Go on, you two. Let me finish up here so I can join you for a visit." Julie turned and went back to work.

"Ok, kiddo, let's go up to the house." Bobbie said as he draped his arm over her shoulder.

"You'll have to give me a couple of minutes, Uncle Bobbie. I have to park my trailer around back, put my truck in the bay and grab my bag. Go on up to the house. I'll be there in a minute."

"Be quick. I have a couple of cold ones waiting for us. We can sit out on the porch and wait for your aunt. Maybe I'll steal another smoke from you before she joins us." He finished with a wink.

THEY WERE STILL SITTING on the porch, enjoying their second beer, when Julie made her way up from the shop. Maggie had grabbed a quick shower first to wash away the road, and her wet hair curled around her face. She had her bare feet draped over the arm of the chair. When Julie went inside to get cleaned up, Bobbie grabbed a couple more beers from the cooler at their feet.

"We might as well enjoy another one. It'll take your aunt a while to get all of that grease off."

Julie called out from the upstairs window. "I heard that."

Bobbie had the good sense to look sheepish as he gave Maggie a wink.

Maggie felt her phone vibrate with a text in her pocket and pulled it out. It was from Adam. 'Are you interested in doing the car shows out west? If so, you'll have to head back to the Port after you deliver and pick up the Porsche's for the shows,' Maggie didn't hesitate. Her fingers flew across the screen. 'I'm in.' Adam replied, 'It's a six-week trip. So, prepare while you're off.'

Maggie squealed with delight. Bobbie waited for Maggie to fill him in as Julie came back out onto the porch.

"They're sending me out west to do the car shows with Porsche." Her face was beaming. "They must think I'm doing a good job, or I wouldn't get the shows."

"How long is this trip?"

"Six weeks! I'll get paid for every waiting day between loading and unloading. What a great gig."

"That's something, isn't it? Good job, sweetie. Maybe you should grab your laundry bag. You'll want to head out with clean clothes."

"Great idea!" Maggie hopped up and sprinted back to the compound to get her laundry bag so she could get her wash started.

Bobbie looked at Julie. "You know, I don't understand why she didn't just bring her laundry up when she arrived."

"I don't think she wants to trouble us. How's supper coming along? Do you need me to set the table?"

"Already done. When Maggie starts her laundry, we can sit down to eat."

MAGGIE SPENT a second night with her aunt and uncle. They completed the oil change first thing the next morning, as her aunt promised. But knowing she'd be away for six weeks; Maggie cleaned the inside of her truck before the tour. It needed a good vacuum. She also went with her uncle to town to pick up supplies for their trucks. This time, Maggie helped her uncle make supper while Julie was at work. It surprised her how much she missed spending time with them. They were both so loving and kind.

'It was unfortunate they couldn't have children. They'd have made great parents.' Maggie thought as she puttered around the kitchen. 'They cared for her and always made time for her. Any child they had would have felt blessed.'

She loved them and knew that moving forward; she'd do better at keeping in contact. They were her surrogate parents, and they deserved better from her.

When it was time to head out, Maggie and her uncle left together. He had a load going to the States, and she had to deliver in Toronto before returning to the Port. As she pulled away, she gave her horn a couple of short toots at her aunt, who stood in the shop's doorway waving them both off. She grinned. Julie was in for a surprise when she ended her day. She and Bobbie had put together a meal in the crock-pot for Julie. It would slow cook all day and be ready for her when she closed up shop.

Uncle Bobbie had taken care of her, too. He'd packed her some sandwiches and made her some meals that she could warm up in the microwave. She was an adult, but it was nice having someone do the little things for you. Her heart warmed at the love she felt. They were such good people; she was lucky to have them. A vision flashed through her mind and she wondered if they'd still feel the same way if they knew everything about her.

26

RYAN

*R*yan pulled into the Flying J in Sault Saint Marie. He'd noticed one of his tarps was flapping, which meant a strap had come loose. Stopping here was earlier than he planned, but he had to fix the strap and secure the tarp before going any further. The guy who'd given him a hand where he'd picked up was more interested in getting out of the rain than securing the load. It didn't matter why it happened; in the end it was his responsibility so he had to fix it.

He chose a spot to back into that was away from the other trucks, so he'd have room to manoeuvre when he secured the load and parked. Ryan hopped out of the cab just as the wind picked up. He cursed under his breath. He'd better hurry if he wanted to get everything locked down and tightened. The wind would make the tarp like a kite caught in a hurricane while he tied it down. At least today it was dry.

He'd have to take his time while he worked at it, tightening one strap at a time, pulling the tarp snug as he went. When he reached the end, he undid the last two straps to reposition the tarp better. A gust of wind caught the tarp, pulling it free. He let out a long line of expletives, then hopped up on his trailer to wrestle with the unwieldy tarp. Before he realized it, the trailer clattered as a tiny woman hopped up beside him and grabbed the other side of the tarp.

"I thought you could use a hand." She stated with a wide grin.

"Thanks, but it's a tough thing to control with this wind."

She jerked her head over her shoulder, motioning to the red Kenworth, and replied, "That's my rig over there. I can tie down a load."

Ryan eyed her up and down. Unable to believe that this tiny woman was a truck driver. But he could see she knew what she was doing, and welcomed the help. He nodded at her as together they got the tarp under control, back in position, and tied down.

Ryan jumped off and offered her a hand, getting down, which she accepted before turning it into a greeting as she shook his hand.

"Hi. I'm Maggie."

"Ryan. Thanks for your help. Why don't we go inside, and you can let me buy you a coffee for your trouble?"

Maggie gave him the once over before agreeing. The wind was whipping through her thin jacket. She'd been on her way inside for a shower. She dropped her bag on the ground, which she bent over to pick up, but a hot coffee would fill the void.

"Sounds great, thank you."

Ryan asked how she took her coffee and ordered, while Maggie found a seat. She told him she had plenty of time to get to her delivery, so she had the time to sit and chat. He made sure she noticed his wedding band and hoped that she was as nice as she seemed.

RYAN PLACED their coffees on the table and sat across from Maggie, his long legs stretched out to the side so that he didn't infringe on her space. He watched as she took a sip of her coffee before he spoke, breaking the silence that hung in the air.

"I have to tell you it was nice of you to help me like that. Very few drivers would've done that."

Maggie smiled before responding.

"I was raised in a family of truckers. Both my father and my uncle spent years behind the wheel, and my aunt is a mechanic. They taught me that the people on the road are our road family, and we need to stick together. I know things have changed a lot since they started, but good manners shouldn't."

"They sound like fine people." Ryan paused and took a sip of his coffee. "It's too bad more people don't think like you. I get it, though, schedules, ELD's everything is working against us. It was different when I first started, just a little over twenty years ago. How long have you been driving?"

"I started about five years ago. First with dry freight, now I haul enclosed vehicles, which I love."

"Sounds like a great gig. What cars do you haul?"

"Mostly high end, but we also do privates. You know, people who buy antique cars or are moving across the country. The company owns the trailer, but the Kenworth is mine."

"So, you're an owner op. How do you like it? I was considering getting a truck of my own, but I haven't bitten the bullet yet."

"I bought my truck as soon as I had my license. Both my dad and my uncle owned their own trucks. It just made sense to me. If you decide to go for it, make sure you know an excellent mechanic. One you can trust. Also, learn how to do some minor work on your own. It can save you a bundle. If my aunt wasn't a mechanic, I'm not sure I would have bought the truck. She doesn't up-charge for parts or charge me labour, as long as I stick around for a visit. If I didn't have her, I would've looked at an older truck, one that was pre-emissions; less problematic, cheaper parts, and if you're so inclined, you can fix a lot on your own."

It impressed Ryan that she was so knowledgeable, even though he felt she was still green to the business. He wondered what the real reason was for her choosing to truck. She was attractive and smart; it wasn't an industry women like her chose. But she was nice to talk to, and the entire conversation wasn't just about trucking.

Maggie and Ryan continued chatting until long after they'd finished their coffees. Ryan asked her about the benefits of being an owner-operator compared to a company driver. The conversation changed, and he talked about his family. Ryan flipped through his phone for her to see pictures of Krissy, Daniel, and Jessica. He beamed as he showed her his family. He was very proud of them.

Maggie pulled her phone out to do the same. She didn't have a husband or kids, but she showed pictures of her parents and aunt and uncle. Ryan paused at the sight of her father. There was something familiar about the smiling man in the baseball cap. But he couldn't put his finger on it, so he said nothing to her, figuring he'd run into him somewhere on the road.

Before they parted, she told Ryan if he bought a truck to contact her. She'd put him in touch with her aunt, who would treat him well if he was in the area. They exchanged numbers, just in case. Plus, it never hurt to have another driver to contact while out on the road. He'd make sure he told Krissy about her when he got back to the truck. No need for her to see Maggie's name on his contact list without a reference point.

Ryan left Maggie to continue on for her shower and returned to his truck. He called Krissy right away and told her about Maggie. She wasn't the jealous type, but secrets, even if they were just omissions, caused problems. He also fired off a quick text to Maggie, thanking her again for her help, then he put his truck in gear and continued on his way.

27

NOELLE

*N*oelle hummed to herself as she wandered through her apartment now that she was home. She sent a warning text to the girl who sublet from her that she was on her way back, that it was time to go, but she still had to kick her out when she first arrived. Now she had the tedious task of cleaning. Noelle wanted nothing of the other girl to remain when she returned to work. She pulled cushions off of her sofa and vacuumed in the crevices. Tiny particles of potato chips crackled up the nozzle. She spent most of the day cleaning the small apartment until it felt like hers again.

Her crisp cotton sheets on her bed would feel good to crawl into tonight. She missed the comfort of her bed, with her nice sheets and fluffy pillows. A whole queen bed to herself, a far cry from the cramped quarters of the trucks she'd been travelling in. But she was home now. The apartment was near to the Husky: a quick bike ride or a short walk if need be. None of her clients knew where she lived, and she kept it that way for the sake of privacy. She never brought a John back here, no matter how much extra they offered.

Satisfied with a job well done, she went out on the balcony to check her bicycle. The tires still held their air, but the chain needed oiling. She could tell that her sublet had used the bike and didn't cover it up. Noelle carried her bicycle up the three flights of stairs every night. Storing it on the balcony, covered with a tarp. She didn't own a car, and this was her primary mode of transportation. Noelle looked after it, so it annoyed her that the girl used it, but didn't cover it.

She found oil for the chain. Then she wiped it down and covered it back up with the tarp. She wouldn't work tonight. Instead, she'd walk over to the grocery store and pick up a few items for her supper. She'd stay in with a movie. It was going to rain anyway, and she still had cash on hand and money in the bank.

She had no one to call to say she was home. She'd grown up in foster care and kicked out the minute she turned eighteen and the money stopped flowing in to support her. There were still a few people she could call, but she didn't have any real friends.

Once in a while, she grabbed drinks with other working girls. But she never got too close. Someone always tried to con her into a place to crash. She didn't mind, but getting them to leave afterwards was the problem. She didn't have a problem going toe to toe with someone to get them out of her home, but bruises and black eyes weren't good for business.

Tomorrow, she'd make her way to the Husky and face whoever moved in on her territory. She just wanted one night of relaxation beforehand. She couldn't face listening to another trucker talk about the growing number of murdered drivers. It was all anyone spoke about now.

28

FRANK

Frank smiled at the thought of being back in his truck. He enjoyed the week at his apartment much to his surprise, but found it limiting. He didn't like people knowing about his business, so he kept to himself. His conning the Super to clean his place had been a stroke of genius. He wasn't sure what kind of rotting mess he'd left. This time, when he departed, he made sure not to leave the trash behind. Frank knew the Super would enter if she suspected a roach infestation and that it stemmed from his place. He wondered if she entered for any other reason, like to snoop!

He'd left Ontario and put the prairies between himself and his time at home. Before he knew it, he was approaching the Husky in Golden, BC, so he pulled in. He needed fuel, a shower, and he was hungry. When he finished fuelling up, he parked his truck, grabbed his shower bag, and headed inside.

The woman at the desk greeted him with a big smile. "Good day. How can I help you?"

Frank eyed her hair in disgust as he noticed the rainbow of hues of her short spiked hair and the sloppy t-shirt she wore to hide her immense bosom.

"I need a shower." He stated, handing her his Husky card in

order to redeem his shower points. He didn't have to pay for a shower when he earned points fuelling up, which was one reason he stopped here. When he finished his shower, he'd go into the restaurant and grab a free meal and use his Husky reward points to pay for that too. He had plenty.

"I have shower one available. Do you need towels?"

Frank nodded. He had a towel, but why dirty his own when theirs were available?

The woman handed him the key and a couple of thread-bare towels. Frank eyed the towels in disgust.

"Would it kill ya to replace these towels?" He barked. "How am I supposed to dry myself with these?" He shook the towels at her, then turned his back and headed to the showers.

"Goddammit!" He cursed as he locked the door behind him. "You'd think with all the money I spend on fuel. They'd have better towels."

He looked around at the dismal room: a toilet, sink, and a curtained shower. There wasn't anywhere to hang his stuff. The hook on the wall had disappeared long ago. At least he didn't shave. He pulled on his long grey beard and chuckled. He could pile everything in the sink and keep it off the floor. Who knows when they cleaned it last?

FRANK FELT frustrated that the shower stall was so small, but at least he was clean and had fresh clothes. He dropped his wet towels in the basket in the hall, returned his key, then made his way into the restaurant for his supper. He picked a booth that faced the door.

"HI, CAN I GET YOU A COFFEE?" The server asked, handing him a menu.

He handed it right back to her. He already knew what he was having.

"I'll take a coffee and the meatloaf dinner with mashed potatoes and gravy."

"Oh, a man who knows what he wants. I like that." She finished with a wink.

He eyed her up and down. He knew she was flirting with him, which he found annoying. Frank realized she wasn't flirting because she liked him; it was for a bigger tip.

'Let's see how fast she is. That will determine whether she gets a tip at all,' Frank muttered under his breath as he shifted in his seat to get a better look at a table with a young family sitting at it.

WHEN HE FINISHED HIS MEAL, he leaned back in the booth and looked around. Some diners had left, including the family, and others had taken their vacant spots. He watched his server scurry after the customers as they arrived. She was well past her prime, but he had to give her credit; she could still move.

'She was quick and attentive.' He thought, *'I guess I'll leave her a couple of bucks.'*

He reached into his pocket and grabbed a couple of loonies, and tossed them on the table. Then he grabbed the bill and headed up to the cash to pay with his points.

He cut through the store on his way out and passed the 'rainbow' lady. She avoided looking at him, so he just scowled at her and made his way out of the building and across the parking lot to his rig. The sun was setting, so he decided he'd spend the night. He didn't have enough hours left on his day to find a parking spot further along the highway. At least here there was a Tim Hortons for his morning coffee fix and a bathroom.

He tossed his bag up into the cab and looked around. The lot was filling up, including the parking spots for truckers on the road. He was lucky he got here when he did. Frank climbed back up into his cab and called it a night. He'd get an early start in the morning.

He pulled the curtains closed to block out the lights from the parking lot and sat back in his chair. Frank's eyes went up to the roof of his cab. Where his ribbon of mementos hung. He reached up and touched the most recent one and sighed.

He allowed his fingers to skim across each of his souvenirs. As his fingers touched them, he remembered when and where he got it and how. His eyes gleamed with a new found purpose. It was time to add another one to his collection.

29

BRANDON, MANITOBA

The man was almost invisible in his hiding spot behind the building. But someone noticed him anyway. A pair of observant eyes watched him from another vantage point, curious why he'd positioned himself that way behind the building beside the garbage bins. The man was long and lean, a contrast to the typical pot-bellied trucker, but that didn't change what he was. He'd pulled his long hair back into a ponytail, and a filthy baseball cap sat low on his forehead, shading his eyes from the sun.

His watcher moved closer, taking cautious steps on the gravel as it ground underfoot to avoid detection. The onlooker wore a plastic rain poncho over jeans and a t-shirt. The killer made a conscious choice to wear it backwards in order for the hood to be pulled up and protect the face from spatter, staying in the shadows, out of sight.

Before taking action, the killer had to be clear about the man's intentions. Soon, long plastic gloves were pulled out and slipped over pale hands as the scene unfolded. Turning from the man to look at the park, where the man's gaze was fixated, waiting to see what transpired, daylight wasn't the best choice, but unavoidable.

The man pulled out his cell phone and held it ready. He faced the playground across the parking lot. His presence remained hidden from all but his potential killer. One hand was ready on his fly. In the playground, a young girl sat on a swing, kicking her legs up and down under her mother's watchful eye. The child's legs pumped with each arch, her pale blue dress fluttered, caught in the gusts of air in the pendulum of forward and backward. Just then, the girl slipped from the swing and ran towards her mother.

"Look, mom," she called out as she cartwheeled across the grass. Her dress flew over her head with each rotation, revealing her white cotton panties as she tumbled over and over.

The man set his phone to the video, recording the child's movements and flash of panties. He shuddered and unzipped his jeans with his free hand. From behind him, anger raged within the witness. The man's true nature now revealed. A hand pulled out a knife and gripped it. There was a sense of satisfaction knowing this man would never succumb to his perversions again.

A few quick steps closed the distance between the watcher and the depraved driver. The gloved hand reached out and sliced across his throat. A faint sound burbled out. His phone dropped from his hand and clattered to the pavement, shattering the screen. He grabbed at his throat, trying in vain to stench the flow of blood. Weakened, he fell forward. His face made a soft, wet sound when it connected with the large metal garbage bin he'd hidden behind. The container shifted forward under the sudden impact as the man crumpled with the last beat of his heart.

The killer took a quick glance around, then removed the plastic gloves and disposable rain poncho, rolled the blood splattered items into a ball. Then a plastic garbage bag was pulled from a front pocket, and the rolled up items were placed inside to be disposed of together to avoid blood contact. Two quick swipes on the man's shirt removed the excess blood from the knife.

The final touch was a small pink plastic child's hair barrette dropped to the ground beside the body. With the job completed and unobserved; the killer slipped off. The evidence tucked away for disposal further down the road.

This wasn't the 'one.' It was never the right 'one', but it was another 'one.' Another sick, twisted pervert attracted to little girls. The world was well rid of him. Soon, the right 'one' would feel the end of his life's blood as it flowed from a knife wound to the neck. Until then, more would die.

30

DR. COLEMAN

*D*r. Coleman leaned over her desk and made notes in her files. Her last patient of the day had left an hour ago, and she was tidying up. When she opened her practice, she began numbering all of her case files to protect her clients. She kept the true identity of each client on an encrypted file, stored on a USB stick that she always carried with her. Audrey did this for two reasons. First. She wanted to guarantee the privacy of all of her clients as many years ago, someone broke into her office looking for drugs. She didn't keep drugs there, but they'd tossed all of her files around and it took forever to sort the mess out. Now she kept the filing cabinet locked. That way, the files within couldn't get into the wrong hands. Being a small community, everybody already knew each other's business, let alone their secrets. The second reason had to do with case 156. 156 had resonated with her, the shadows of this client's trauma had stayed with her as it echoed something from her own past. She felt protective of 156, no matter how dark the thoughts of this patient may be. Audrey understood she had to protect 156 at all costs.

She leaned backward and stretched. Audrey raised her arms above her head and backward so that her back arched in the chair.

She looked around her office. Audrey had a welcoming sofa, as sometimes clients believed they should lie down during their sessions, but her last client always chose the armchair across from her desk. She had a small selection of props for her younger clients. It helped them to play-act situations rather than to discuss them, especially if someone hurt them.

She looked at the framed photo on her desk. There was an identical one at home on her bedside table; she'd taken the photograph many years ago, before everything in her life changed, which was why she wasn't in it. It was a picture of her smiling daughter, who was only eight when she died. Her daughter sat on her husband's lap, with both smiling at her behind the camera. It was the last photo ever taken of the two of them. Only a few weeks later, they were both dead, and everything shifted.

But it was a lifetime ago when she had dark hair. Now age and time had turned her hair silver. She never remarried. The void created when she lost them was something that left her shattered, unable to open her heart. Instead, she devoted herself to her clients.

In the aftermath, she sought her own counselling. After that, she headed back to school and became a psychiatrist. She returned to her hometown and set up practice. She couldn't live in the city surrounded by the violence and dangers that lurked around every corner. Once she had her degree, she packed up her old life, placed a few things in storage, and moved into her cottage.

Being alone, she only needed a small space to live and the year-round cottage was on the water and it fit the bill. She'd picked a small office in town for her practice, and she kept the two very separate. She never brought a file home. The only exception was the USB, which she took home every night and kept hidden.

She gathered up her files, put them away, and locked the filing cabinet. Audrey scanned and saved all of her additional notes to the USB and transferred the day's recordings to the proper files. She could have keyed everything into her computer, but something was satisfying and inspiring about writing her notes by hand. It allowed her to reflect on the nuances she had picked up on during the sessions.

She dropped the USB stick into her purse and prepared to head home when her phone rang. She paused and thought she'd just let the service answer it. They'd tell her if the call was important. But she looked at the call display. The number belonged to 156. Without thinking, she reached for the phone.

"Hello, 156."

"Hi, Dr. Coleman."

"I've told you to call me Audrey. I'm not your doctor anymore."

"Ok, Audrey then." Silence followed.

"Is everything ok?" Audrey asked. 156 wouldn't call so late just to chat.

"I keep having flashbacks to what happened. I've tried to control the rage within me, but I think I'm failing."

"What do you mean, failing? Do you have something to tell me?"

"No. I can't say anything just yet. If I need to, I will. I guess I wanted to hear your voice. It's so soothing." 156 sighed.

"Do you remember to use your coping strategies?"

"Yes, Audrey." 156's voice dropped to almost a whisper.

"Keep practicing them. When will you be here again? I could squeeze you in if you have need for a face-to-face."

"You don't have to worry, Audrey. You helped me heal. I moved forward. Whatever happens or doesn't happen now, it's not your fault."

The line went dead.

"156? 156!" Audrey dialled the number back. But it passed straight to voice mail.

"Something's wrong," Audrey muttered to the air.

She sat staring at the phone, willing it to ring again while knowing it wouldn't. 156 wasn't spiralling out of control; the voice that spoke to her was in full control, but something was going on.

She waited another half hour in her office in case 156 called back. She resolved herself that the phone wouldn't ring again and got up, locked up her office, and headed home. Blue and Ash were waiting for her to feed them, and she needed a drink.

31

MAGGIE

$\mathcal{W}$ith the cars delivered to the convention centre in Vancouver, Maggie headed to Chilliwack. She found Josh parked at the rear of the lot, waiting for her. He'd disconnected the cab of his truck from his trailer and moved it to the space next to his so he could save her a spot. She saw JD's truck parked on the other side of Josh's cab and the thought of his crazy antics brought a smile to her face. It looked like they were going to make a truck sandwich out of her. They were on the car tour together and would need to park here for 12 days, and it was their only option while they waited for the car show to finish.

The first 7 days would cover the length of the show and the next five days were because they had time to waste before they picked up their loads, ready to be delivered in Edmonton. They didn't want to leave before they had to. Chilliwack's weather promised to be in the double digits, while Edmonton was expecting a snowstorm. It was better to enjoy warm rain rather than freezing snow, plus everything they needed was within walking distance.

As soon as Josh saw her pull in, he moved his cab out of the way and parked it in front of his trailer so that she could back into the spot between himself and JD. She laughed when she realized she was going to be in between them. Was it their idea of a joke? Monkey in the middle? No, she realized, they had their protective mode running. They were her father's age. It didn't matter what the reason was; Maggie enjoyed spending time with them both. She enjoyed the family camaraderie they shared.

She hadn't seen Josh since the Road King in Calgary when Tom was with them, and it had been months since she had seen JD.

As she backed up, she noticed JD jumped in front of her truck and made a goofy face. She smiled and waved at him as she pulled the brake and climbed down. She ran to give him a big squeeze. He wrapped her in his arms and lifted her off the ground. Then swung her around in a bear hug to the sound of her laughter.

"Ok, JD, put her down. If you're not careful, you'll break her. Maggie's just a wee thing." Josh called out as he made his way over.

"I may be small, but I'm mighty." Maggie retorted as he approached. "Did you get everything squared away with little mama?"

At first Josh looked puzzled before he remembered what had happened the last time he saw her. "Oh ya, changing your Facebook status helped. Thanks for that."

JD went back to his truck and returned, tossing them both a beer.

"Works over for the day. We'll set up your trailer as our central Mags. Josh and I picked up stuff for all of us for dinner. We thought we'd BBQ later. I think the Totter gang is also on the tour, so they might join us for drinks."

Maggie smiled as she popped open her beer and took a quick sip. She'd noticed that there were several Totter trucks in the lot when she pulled in. She wondered if one belonged to Tammy. They'd hit it off on the last tour they were all on and had kept in contact since. It would be nice to have another female driver around to chat with.

They set up the folding chairs in the back of Maggie's trailer. Both Josh and JD brought over coolers filled with ice and beer. Maggie unhooked her camp table from the side of the trailer and dug out her BBQ.

"I think I'll walk over to the liquor store and get some beer." Maggie contemplated out loud.

"Don't worry about it. We've got you covered. When you go, just toss it in with ours. We can all pull from the coolers. You know it always works out in the end. Besides, we figured we bought the stuff for dinner, so you'd cook it." JD finished with a chuckle and a wink.

Soon, the Totter guys joined them, and as luck would have it, Tammy was there too. Everyone set up their chairs in Maggie's trailer. They needed to be discrete about drinking in the parking lot. Plus, it protected them all if the weather turned. The night continued as laughter echoed from inside the trailer.

32

NOELLE

The sun was still high in the sky with the promise of a warm night when Noelle rode into the Husky parking lot. The first thing she noticed when she arrived was that the car haulers had taken over the back row. She saw one truck belonged to one of her regulars, but knew she wouldn't be visiting him tonight. He'd want her to stay away when he was with his crew. It was too bad; he was one of her favourites. She wondered how long they'd be here. From the looks of things, it appeared they'd be here a while. She saw the smoke from the BBQs' cooking and where the group had congregated.

She looked up as Maggie stepped down from her truck. They'd all parked around her. Noelle tsked to herself.

'They're like flies to honey, where she's concerned.' Noelle muttered under her breath. 'I'll keep away from the back row. There are plenty of other trucks here for me to visit.'

She began her well-practiced moves on her bicycle as she rode past each truck. It was still early, with lots of vacant spots, but she wasn't worried. Although Noelle found it unusual that no one had signalled her over yet. She hated the idea of knocking on doors, asking if anyone wanted company. Noelle felt it degraded her. She'd worked at this stop for so many years that she'd become a fixture. The owners didn't even bother with her anymore. In the beginning, they'd shoo her away, but they knew she wasn't hurting anyone and turned a blind eye.

She'd almost given up hope when a set of lights flashed from an interested driver. Noelle rode to the truck. The man leaned out of the window, waiting to talk to her.

"How much?" He called out.

Noelle pulled closer. "Why don't we discuss that inside? If we don't agree on the terms, I'll leave."

He checked her out before motioning for her to get in. She locked her bicycle to his bumper and climbed up into the passenger side. 'How much' depended on what he wanted. It was bad for business to talk about the terms of her services where someone could hear them. She never knew if a cop was in the area.

Noelle and the driver talked until they agreed on the rate and service, and she began another night's work.

33

RYAN

R yan listened to the phone ring while he waited for Krissy to answer.

"I love you today," he said when she picked up.

Her soft laughter filled his ears.

"And I love you today."

"I wanted to let you know I'll be home tomorrow, but after that, I'll be going first to Nova Scotia and then straight to BC. The weather's getting cooler, so I'm going to change out some of my clothes. I heard there was already snow in the prairies. Can you believe it?"

"Snow this early in the year? If you're heading to BC, do you have your chains?"

"I always have them. I keep the chains attached to the headache rack at the back of my cab." Ryan finished with a chuckle.

"Looks like I'd better run to the store. Let me know what you'll need. I realize the basics, but what else? By the sound of it, you'll be away a few weeks." Krissy mumbled while putting her phone on speaker so that she could create a list in her notes. "Oh, and I'll run your winter gear through the wash today so that it's fresh for you to take."

"Thanks' sweetie. Let me think. Milk, bread, chips, a box of

Cheerios, and some gummy bears. Oh, I'm also almost out of peanut butter, instant rice, and oatmeal."

"Got it. I'll make a beef stew in the crock-pot tomorrow so we can prepare some more meals for you. I noticed you were running low."

"You're the best! I'll see you at home. Baby, I've got to go. I'm almost at my delivery. I love you."

"Love you too, baby."

Ryan pressed the button to disconnect the Bluetooth. He was thankful that Krissy paid attention to the details, such as when he was running low on the meals in the freezer. She always cooked extra and made sure that Ryan ate well-balanced meals on the road. His truck had a fridge and microwave, so he just warmed up a meal at the end of his day and only ate out if he ran out. Sometimes he'd grabbed some frozen meals from the grocery store, but they weren't the same.

He was glad that dispatch gave him the heads up for the extended trip this time. Now he'd fill a cooler with food as well. Krissy froze his dinners, so he ate whatever thawed first. It didn't matter how many meals he brought, he'd still wind up buying a few on the road. He'd stop at a grocery store before he ran out. He needed to make sure that he always had meals on board. There was no guarantee he'd end his day near a restaurant.

He arrived at his delivery and pulled out his coat off the hook. It was drizzling, and he wanted to stay as dry as possible. He still had to undo the straps and fold up his tarps, but a crane would take his load off the trailer. When his load came off, he'd head back to the yard and then home.

34

FRANK

he check engine light flickered on Frank's dash as he crossed the border into Windsor. He banged his fist on the console and the light went out. He figured there was something wrong with the bulb or the wiring to the bulb, since his truck was running well. His trip had been productive in more ways than one. He had racked up lots of miles, which meant more money in his pocket, but he also got a new souvenir, which he'd fastened to the end of the ribbon of mementos. The ribbon was over two feet long, but there wasn't much room left on it. Maybe he needed a longer ribbon.

He thrust his chest out as he thought about how he got this one. Finding the perfect souvenir always took time. Frank didn't buy them. No, he took them. There was no satisfaction in buying a souvenir. It was the conquest that went with the acquisition that mattered. He'd been at it for so many years, and so far, he'd escaped detection. He was always careful, kept to the outskirts, and struck quickly. The trick was to keep to himself and the fact that he travelled the highways across Canada and the US helped. He smiled with a slight sneer.

He realized he'd have to wait before taking another, no matter how tempting it became. If he became too cocky, he wouldn't continue to get away with it. Frank knew he'd have to be careful. He was a patient man, as luck would have it. He would have to allow the memory of his success to fuel his need for now.

Frank stroked his beard as he relived the search in his mind. The game of cat and mouse, until he found his mark and succeeded. Hunting for the perfect specimen was exhilarating; almost as much as the conquest. He wouldn't look again for months. He could sate his hunger with mental imagery while he held the ribbon. In the meantime, the keepsakes and memories would suffice.

He glanced at his clock and realized he was running out of hours. It looked like he'd only make it to London. That was ok. By then, he'd be hungry, anyway. His load went to Thunder Bay. After that, he'd do his mandatory 36-hour re-set, load up and head to Vancouver. The more distance he put between himself and Detroit, the better.

He reached out and turned on his satellite radio, picked Prime Country, and continued along the 401 in what was its deadliest corridor. The carnage left along this stretch of the highway made it unpredictable. He'd have to watch for idiots until he could stop for the night.

35

DR. COLEMAN

*H*er shoulders drooped and her lower back ached as she entered her home. She leaned forward, trying to stretch her tight muscles. Her work day had been exhausting and left her drained, then to top it off there was the call from 156. She was glad to be home, surrounded by the peace and tranquillity of her cottage.

Ash wove around her ankles and let out a mournful meow, showing his hunger as Audrey popped open a couple of cans of food. Blue joined him and her cats purred as they intertwined in her legs. If her husband was still alive, he would have preferred a dog, but they were more work. You had to walk a dog, and she found her emotions drawn taut when she got home. Cats were ok being home alone all day and seemed to prefer it. They used a litter box, but still cuddled with her in front of the TV. It was the cuddling that she enjoyed, the physical contact with something living. It made her home less lonely.

She reached up to her wine rack, something she'd fastened to the wall by the cabinets because the floor space was small, and selected a bottle. Before she left this morning, she'd started a beef stroganoff in the crock-pot. The rich aromas greeted her when she walked through the door, and her stomach rumbled in anticipation.

She picked a Malbec to enjoy with her meal. Under normal circumstances, she ate at the table, which she still set for three, even though two spots remained empty. But after talking to 156, she needed to distract herself, so she pulled out her tv tray and sat down in front of the television. She'd find an old episode of CSI or Criminal Minds for entertainment while she ate.

She settled on the sofa as Ash and Blue hopped up and curled up on either side of her as she took a sip of her wine. The steaming bowl of stroganoff on rice sat in front of her. Audrey allowed her mind to drift back to her brief conversation with 156. Her brow furrowed as she took another sip.

'I know something is going on. It wasn't just the words; it was the tone of voice.' She thought. *'I think I'll pull up the case file and review it in the morning. Maybe I missed some triggers or warning signs. I'll go in early so that I can do it before my first client arrives.'*

She ate without tasting her dinner, as her mind kept drifting back to the conversation. When she finished, she put the dishes in the dishwasher and poured herself a second glass. It was unusual for her to drink two or more, but she had so much on her mind she needed the extra glass to calm herself. She also hoped it would help her sleep. Not too much wine though, or she'd find herself wide awake in the middle of the night and she'd have trouble falling back to sleep.

With a cat on either side of her, she relaxed as she stroked them. The vibrations of their purrs soothed her frazzled nerves in a way the wine could never do. Images of the show continued to flicker across the screen until she dozed. The stress of the day was long forgotten as she fell into a deep slumber.

36

MAGGIE

The sun peaked through the curtains in Maggie's truck. She blinked, realizing it was daylight. She grabbed her phone and squinted. 7 am. She debated rolling over and grabbing a few more minutes, but dismissed the idea. Instead, she slipped out from beneath the covers, threw on a pair of jeans and a t-shirt, grabbed her toiletry kit, and headed to the washroom.

The women's washroom was empty, so she took her time. She washed her face, brushed her teeth and smoothed her hair back into a neat ponytail, figuring she'd grab a shower later after her morning walk. A ball cap completed the look as she headed back to her truck to put away her bag. Then she went around to the trailer to grab her bundle buggy. The guys made fun of her for using it, but when she was in Chilliwack, she walked 10 kilometres every day. It was easier if she rolled her purchases behind her instead of loading up each arm. Her shoulders would ache if she carried everything she bought.

Her first stop was the B.C. Liquor store. She'd grab a box of red and some beer to replace what she drank. The boxed wine may not be classy, but it wouldn't break, and it would stay fresh after opening. Plus, the box would fit at the bottom of the buggy.

She continued up Vedder Road to Fraser Valley Meats. They had the best grass-fed, grass-finished meats she'd ever tasted. Tonight, she was in charge of dinner, so she grabbed some bacon-wrapped, mesquite rubbed, pork medallions. Maggie also picked up a bag of Greek potatoes for the dinner and blueberry sausage for her breakfast tomorrow.

She debated going to the Safeway but opted for the Superstore for the rest of her groceries. On her way, she'd stop to have a coffee at Tim Hortons. One thing she liked about this Superstore was they allowed you to buy individual vegetables. So, if she wanted one celery stick, she could get it, which was handy when food storage was at a premium, as in the truck.

Her buggy was so full it couldn't hold anymore, but her errands were done, so she headed back to her truck. She'd put her purchases away and see where everyone else was.

MAGGIE DIDN'T HAVE to look far. She started walking to the trailer to put away the bundle buggy and add the beer she bought to the cooler when she heard laughter coming from inside. She popped her head through the open doors and looked in. Sitting in the chairs, she found Josh, JD, and the group from Totter trading stories. She pulled out her phone to discover that she'd been away for over four hours.

"Get in here, girl." One of the Totter guys called out as he pulled a chair closer.

Maggie took the last items out of her buggy. She held up the box of wine in one hand and the case of beer in the other.

"How far behind you all am I?"

JD held up his can of beer. "Not far. I'm only on my first beer."

"If JD is only on his first, we're just getting started." Josh cut in.

Maggie laughed. "I'll sit down and have a drink with you all, but I'm cooking tonight, so for all of our sakes, I'll limit it to one. After we eat, all bets are off."

"What are you cooking, Mags?" Tammy asked.

Maggie told her what she'd picked up from Fraser Valley Meats and the rest of the menu. She even picked up an apple pie for dessert.

Tammy turned to her crew. "That sounds like a great menu. I'll run out and get the same for whoever wants to join in. Just toss me some money to contribute."

Tammy collected cash from the others in her group and swung back to Maggie.

"Can I borrow your buggy? It'll make my trip easier."

"Of course, Tammy." Maggie smiled.

Tammy twisted back to her fellow drivers and suggested that they gather whatever BBQs they had between them and bring them over. Tonight, they'd have a cookout.

37

NOELLE

$\mathcal{N}$oelle rode into the parking lot and swung past the car haulers when she arrived at the Husky. The savoury aroma of cooked meat filled her nostrils, reminding her she hadn't eaten today. She could hear the laughter coming from one trailer in the group, and she felt a pang of jealousy.

It had been a long time since she had real friends to hang out with. Her line of work wasn't conducive to friendships. She worked nights, and most women stayed clear of her as if she was a pariah. Noelle understood the score and had learned to deal with it. It only bothered her in situations like this where she could hear others having fun.

She continued riding until she cleared her head and started along the second row of trucks when her regular, Todd from the Totter group, caught up with her.

"Hey, Noelle. I told everyone that I'd grab a shower." He held up his travel bag. "Why don't you join me? I'll make it worth your while."

She shrugged her shoulders and thought, *'Why not?'*

She'd have to clean up afterwards anyway, so showering would be double duty.

"Sure, you realize you're my favourite." She purred.

His grin cracked across his pale face. "I'll meet you inside."

Noelle still had to secure her bicycle anyway, so she nodded. He didn't want anybody to see him with her. He wanted her, but didn't want anyone to see them together, and she understood that. She knew his group made fun of her. They called her Ten Speed. The derogatory term didn't bother her. It could refer to her bike or something else. There could be several meanings. In her line of work, she needed a thick skin.

She secured her bike to the huge brown garbage receptacle. It wasn't collection day, so she didn't have to worry about the trash collectors coming by, and it was too large for someone to move just to steal her bicycle.

She entered the store just as Todd walked into shower 1. He gave her a wink before closing the door. She made her way through the small convenience store. She looked up at the cashier to make sure she wasn't looking before she slipped inside to join him.

WHEN THEY FINISHED, Todd left first. He wanted to be certain no one watched when she left. The store was empty, so he walked up to the cashier to return the dirty towels to the bin and distract her while Noelle snuck out.

She saw Todd talking with the clerk and she left the building. She whistled as she unlocked her bike, then she noticed a set of lights flashing at her. Instead, she relocked the bike and left it there. No one would bother with it or know which truck she was visiting. Maybe she'd leave her bike here from now on, except on garbage collection days. She shook her head, wondering why she hadn't thought of it before. At least it was here, available for a quick get-a-way if she needed one.

38

RYAN

A thin waft of snow skipped along Highway 1 as Ryan pulled off the road to park for the night. He looked up at the darkened sky and knew a storm was coming. He pulled off the road early to find a place to park now rather than risk going further. When a snow storm cut across the prairies, the highway proved treacherous; the wind cut across the flats, creating white-out conditions and havoc for all drivers.

He wasn't getting stuck on the highway. A few years ago, a storm closed the road for a couple of days. It took forever to get things moving. Good Samaritans used snowmobiles to bring food and coffee to the stranded motorists. Krissy had gone ballistic on him when she discovered he was stuck in that mess. He had to promise that he'd always pay attention to the weather and make safer choices where possible. There was no need for him to cause his family to worry.

He knew that staying at the Husky in Brandon, Manitoba, even if he was storm-stayed, he could at least get fuel and food while he waited it out. Ryan pulled into the fuel bay to fill up his tanks before he found a spot. With the temperatures dropping, he might have to keep the truck running or he'd have trouble starting it. It was something he'd have to keep his eye on. Ryan was lucky and found a spot in the front row, close to the building. He didn't want to walk further than he needed to in a blizzard. By morning he knew he'd find trucks parked anyway they could, they'd squeeze in if things got as bad as predicted. He hoped they didn't park two-deep in front of the pumps, or he'd have trouble getting out in the morning if the weather looked promising.

SNUG IN HIS TRUCK, Ryan cranked up the bunk heater. Wind whipped through the thin insulation of the cab, creating a draft, and with his thin frame he felt the cold. The last time he peered out through his curtains, he noticed that two feet of snow had already accumulated on the ground. The plows were out clearing the roads, but it looked like a losing battle.

He turned up his CB for the latest road condition reports. It wasn't long before he learned that, as he expected, a significant accident had taken place in the westbound lanes of Highway 1, blocking all traffic. He moved to his driver's seat and looked out of the window and observed the growing line of traffic.

It wasn't long before when he looked out and saw there was chaos on the road. The highway had become a parking lot. Trucks were in ditches, emergency personnel and plows had difficulty getting through. He wondered if he should go out and try to help, but thought better of it. He'd be on foot, which would limit what he could do. Tim Hortons and Husky were just off the highway for any drivers stuck close by.

The temperature had dropped 10 degrees since he parked. The bunk heater wasn't enough anymore, and he started his truck. It was the primary reason he'd fuelled up before parking. He heard the engines running in the trucks next to him, so he turned his key. The engine started after a brief hesitation under protest of the negative temperatures. He leaned back in his seat and decided it was time to warm up his supper in the microwave.

In the morning, he'd have to call dispatch and inform them of the situation here. He hoped the roads would open, but if not, that it would only take a couple of days, so he'd still make his delivery on time.

Next, he'd call Krissy. He realized she'd be watching the weather reports, and although she understood he'd parked for the night, she'd want to learn the status of the highways and his travel plans. He loved how she worried about him, but didn't want her to worry needlessly.

After turning on the microwave, he made his phone calls and settled in for the duration. He thumbed through his collection of DVDs until he found one that looked interesting and sat back to watch while he ate his dinner.

39

FRANK

Frank cursed at the snow that swirled around his rig and the situation in which he found himself. He should have stopped in Brandon; but he wanted to get more miles in. He thought he'd make it. Now he was stuck in a massive traffic jam. Somewhere up ahead, a rig slid across the highway and blocked both lanes. He didn't know the number of cars involved, but he'd heard it was immense.

Frank glanced at the fuel gauge. It registered at 3/4's of a tank. He'd be fine, as long as the storm didn't last too long. Static from his CB broke the silence as drivers continued to report on the storm and the number of accidents. He'd had enough, so he reached up and turned off his CB. There was no reason to listen to the chatter anymore. He had no choice but to stay put until they got things moving. Frank parked his truck and grabbed something to eat from the back.

Frank had a small freezer compartment in his fridge, and although he ate in restaurants, he always kept a couple of frozen TV dinners in there, just in case. He pulled one out and popped it in the microwave to warm up.

While it cooked, he prepared his coffee pot. He'd want a hot coffee in the morning. There was nowhere around where he could buy one. He grabbed a bottle of coke and put it on the passenger seat, ready to wash down his meal. Soon the microwave dinged, signalling that his supper was ready. He put the hot tray on a plastic plate and sat back in the driver's seat to eat his supper and watched the events play out on the road ahead.

He watched the swirling snow drift up against the vehicles ahead of him. This storm was a bad one. It might take a few days for rescuers to dig everyone out. He sighed, relieved that he had tons of snacks on board. There were only three of four meals, but these snacks would keep his hunger at bay.

He dumped the empty dinner tray into the garbage and took a long pull on his pop. It was a good thing he emptied his pee jug at his last stop. Frank didn't know what the four-wheelers would do, not that he cared. They could fend for themselves just like he had to do. All he cared about was that he was dry and comfortable.

He swivelled his seat to face his bunk and pick up the remote to turn on the TV. He wasn't sure if he'd get a reception. The drone of the TV and grey snow on the screen confirmed his suspicions. "Fuck." He yelled into the air. Frank switched the channel to DVD and started one disc from the multipack DVD on the disc drive. He'd view a movie to pass the time. There were hours of movies to choose from.

The one that started was an old Clint Eastwood western, one of his favourites. He hauled down a bag of chips to munch on while he watched. He still had plenty of pop left in the bottle, so he'd continue to drink it until it was gone.

When the show ended, he shut off the TV, and looked out at the snowy roads before he went to bed. He pulled out his jug to relieve himself and got into the bunk, not bothering to remove his clothes. If they opened the highway, the cops would bang on his door to get him to move. He wanted to be dressed and ready, just in case.

40

DR. COLEMAN

The phone in the office rang just as Audrey finished her lunch. The caller ID identified the caller as 156. It had been a few weeks since they last spoke. Ever since, Audrey had paid close attention to the news and learned they were looking for a serial killer. 156 could be in trouble, but Audrey wasn't sure.

"Hello?"

"Hello, Audrey. It still doesn't feel right to use your first name."

Audrey chuckled. "Give it time. You'll get used to it. Tell me what's on your mind 156?"

"I'm sure you've been listening to the news."

"I always listen to the news." Audrey exclaimed. "Are you referring to anything in particular?" She asked, hoping 156 would give her a clue what was going on and if there was anything for her to worry about.

"The serial killer, Audrey." The voice lowered to almost a whisper.

"What do you know about that?" Even as she asked, she sensed she wouldn't get the truth. "Do you think you're in danger?"

"Audrey," there was a pause, "whoever is doing this, it seems they are doing the world a favour."

Audrey paused. "What do you mean?"

"Every truck driver killed so far has been a deviant." 156 explained.

"How can you be certain?" Audrey frowned.

"Driver's talk. It's all over the CB. They're saying one guy had pictures of little girls on his phone and a video recording of a young girl at play when someone killed him. And get this, his dick was out, and it was broad daylight. How much proof do they need? The victims are all scum," 156 concluded.

The silence hung across the line. Audrey waited for 156 to talk again. She sighed, knowing 156 wouldn't be a victim. But the revelation didn't eliminate any potential involvement. Audrey had been careful while she reviewed the case file for 156.

"Did you hear me?" 156 asked.

"Yes, I did. Good riddance to bad rubbish, I always say. Can you promise me you're not involved?"

"I'm surprised you'd even ask that after all that we've been through together. I don't have sympathy for the victims. It's almost as if we should relish the news. We both understand how deadly sexual deviants can be," 156 retorted.

"Yes, we do."

"I'll call you in a couple of weeks. Bye."

"Bye 156."

When the line cut off, Audrey stared at the receiver in her hand and realized that 156 had avoided answering her question.

41

EDMUNDSTON, N.B.

The killer stood back and remained hidden in the shadows, watching the man as he left the casino. Even from this distance, the swagger gave away the victim's identity. His unmistakable confidence blurred with the effects of alcohol as he returned to his rig.

THE DRUNKEN MAN spent the better part of the night inside the casino, drinking and playing the slots. In his arrogance, he was oblivious to the people around him as he spoke to his companion, his tongue loosened by his intoxication.

"I guess there might be something to this child bride thing in other countries." He laughed, elbowing his friend in the ribs. "Think about it. You could train them to act and be what you want. They'd be virgins, and you'd know no one else had been there before you."

"You know that's sick, right?" His friend questioned.

"What? You've never considered it?" The man retorted.

"No, nothing is appealing about having a child bride. I like tits on my women, great big ones. Not a flat-chested kid."

The first fellow realized his blunder and attempted to cover up his hasty words and deep-seated desires.

"Oh, I don't mean that children are attractive. It's just the idea of having a wife to train to do what I want and who hasn't been with anyone else. That's all I meant by that. I don't want an actual child." He spit the words out, hoping he'd covered up his true nature.

He noticed his companion eyed him with suspicion as he shifted his seat further away. His friend was acting as if he was a leper. He couldn't shake the feeling that he'd said too much. The man thought of his companion as a friend, but now he realized he pushed the boundaries too far. He was thankful to be going back to his truck and heading in a different direction. Maybe the alcohol would blur his memory and he'd forget.

Unbeknownst to the two men, someone else had overheard their conversation. Someone whose fists curled with rage. Someone who couldn't let another pervert survive; this person slipped out of the casino early to lay and wait. Patience was a rewarding game, and practice led to perfection.

THE DAMP NIGHT air was heavy with drizzle, tonight the rain poncho wouldn't appear suspicious. The diligence of waiting proved fruitful as the prey exited the building. He was alone, as his friend had left long ago to return to his own rig. The assailant watched. The man stumbled across the parking area as he made his way up the hill to the road where he'd parked his truck. Shadowy darkness from the misty night along the roadway would provide the perfect cover.

The killer slipped out and slunk along the row of trucks in the Grey Rock parking lot. Eyes locked onto the next victim, following him as he went. Unsure which truck the man was heading to, the pursuer kept low, crouched close to the grass along the slight incline to the line of parked trucks. Darkness would cover the violence that would end the man's life.

The blade grasped in the right hand, ready to be used. This death had to be quick. The parking lot was still busy, with truckers coming and going. If the killer took too long to strike, there could be a potential witness, and that couldn't happen.

The man stopped between his truck and trailer, and the killer seized the opportunity. The knife slashed his throat, gurgles expelled from his mouth, which was full of bubbles of blood, before he collapsed on the pavement. It only took a few minutes for the killer to tuck the blade inside the bundle made of the disposable raincoat and veterinary gloves, and stuffed everything into a hoodie pocket. A left fist, clenched throughout the assault, released the pink plastic hair clip and tossed it onto the body.

The killer sprinted across the grassy knoll before sauntering along the sidewalk, dealing with the evidence to be disposed of at a later time. It was too public here. A sense of euphoria spread through the killer, knowing another deviant had met his end.

KIDNAPPED

4 2

DETECTIVE TATE

𝒞olby's phone chirped with a text notifying him they'd found another victim, this time in Edmundston, N.B. Because they'd linked the cases together, the local officers had a heads up and reported it immediately to the RCMP. They taped off the scene and took detailed photographs of the body and its placement before shipping the corpse off to the morgue. An officer would remain at the scene until Colby could arrive. He caught the next flight out, eager to review fresh evidence instead of the old case files.

His pulse raced. This was the first fresh crime scene he was going to examine since they determined they were dealing with a serial killer. So far, they'd been lucky, and although the journalists somehow got wind that there was a serial killer, they hadn't discovered the key piece of evidence linking the cases together. Colby assumed it had something to do with the victims; all men, all truck drivers who lived a transient lifestyle. If the fatalities fit another demographic, it would have been front page news. One thing they'd been careful about was the pink barrette left at the scene, Colby was certain that was the clue to catching their killer, but he wasn't one hundred percent sure of the significance.

THERE WAS an officer waiting for him at the airport and transported him to the crime scene. The care the local police force had taken in preserving the evidence and crime scene impressed him. The officer in charge strode over to greet him.

"Hi Detective Tate, I'm Lance Bowman." He reached out to shake Colby's hand. "Let me fill you in on what we've learned so far."

Colby followed Bowman to the cordoned off area. The first thing he noticed was that there were cones set up on one side of the truck, blocking off a lane of traffic. There was tape surrounding the truck. The victim's blood pooled between the tractor and the trailer. Bowman took the lead.

"It seems our VIC was in the casino drinking most of the night. We've determined this because we reviewed the surveillance tapes from inside the building and spoke to witnesses who saw him there. He was sitting with someone he appeared friendly with. We don't have an I.D. on the other man yet, but we are working on it."

Colby looked down the hill towards the casino. He noted the distance from the truck and the seclusion offered based on where they found the body.

"Is this the VIC's truck?"

"Yes. The VIC's name is Yousaf Kalid, 46, and he's not from New Brunswick. His company is from out of Ontario. We have already notified the local department so that they can notify next of kin."

Colby peered down at the congealed mass of blood on the pavement where the victim bled out before he turned to search the lamp posts for security cameras. There weren't any. They still classified the road as unassumed, because the city hadn't taken it over from the casino.

"Let me guess. No one heard or saw anything."

"Nope. Another driver found the victim before he pulled away. The driver, Mark Zwicker, stopped when he saw the body and called it in. He's being very cooperative. We're lucky he didn't just call in an anonymous tip. Most truckers won't bother getting held up in a murder investigation. It cuts into their driving time and money earned."

"You seem to know a lot about truckers, Lance."

"Ya, well, my brother-in-law is one. It's freaking out my sister that someone is killing truckers. This one will hit too close to home."

"Is your brother-in-law a solid guy?" Colby waited while Lance nodded. "Then tell your sister I don't think she has anything to worry about. I'm working on a theory, and good guys don't figure into the victimology. Tell me, was there a hair clip near the body?"

Lance's jaw slacked as he gaped at Colby. "Yes, a little pink plastic one. How did you know?"

"So far, we've found one at every crime scene. We're assuming the killer left it." Colby replied.

Colby continued taking notes and pictures of the crime scene before going over to speak with the driver, who'd called it in. He wanted to allow the driver to get moving, but needed his statement first.

When he had completed everything he needed to do at the scene, he headed to the station with the investigating officers to review the photos of the body's position. His last stop would be the coroner's before he headed back to Halifax to report to his superiors.

43

MAGGIE

$\mathcal{M}$aggie heard a knock on her truck as she rubbed sleep from her eyes. She rolled over and stretched, hoping whoever it was would go away.

"Get up, lazybones!" JD called out. "Josh and I are heading in for breakfast. Come join us."

Maggie threw on an oversized T-shirt, hopped out of bed, and peered out of the window.

"Ok, keep your pants on JD. Give me a couple of minutes, OK? Go in and order me a coffee. I won't be long."

JD chuckled. "No problem. We'll go in and get some seats. Don't be too slow, or your coffee will get cold." JD stepped away from the rig and joined Josh as they made their way to the restaurant.

Maggie grabbed some baby wipes to freshen herself up with before she finished getting dressed. She'd shower a little later in the day. Maggie slipped into a pair of jeans and a tank top, ran a brush through her hair, and pulled it back into a ponytail. Then she took a quick swirl of mouth wash and spat it into an empty water bottle before pulling on her cowboy boots. The last things she picked up was her wallet and sunglasses before she left her rig.

Maggie looked down the row of trucks to where Tammy had

parked. She hesitated. Maybe she should ask Tammy to join them. Then she noticed that Tammy's husband had parked beside her. A smile crept across her lips. No, she better not disturb them. She'd catch up with Tammy when Kevin moved on, unless they joined them in the trailer later. Tammy and Kevin worked for the same company but drove separate from each other. Maggie shook her head. She couldn't imagine how hard it was having a husband you didn't see. That's why she stayed single. It was best to give them some privacy. If they joined the rest of the group later, that would be fine.

Maggie slipped her sunglasses on and made her way through the rows of trucks in the parking lot to the Husky restaurant. Her stomach rumbled as she got closer and she realized she was hungry.

MEANWHILE, JD glanced up at the clock on the wall. He felt Maggie was taking a long time. He'd already drank her coffee and was preparing to order her a fresh one.

"I'm going to see what's keeping Maggie." He said as he stood up.

Josh chuckled. "I'm sure she'll be along soon. You know you could call or text her."

JD grinned. "Ya, but I've got to take a piss, anyway. While I'm there, I'll look out and see if she's coming. If not, we can call her. Maybe she fell back to sleep. She put back a lot of wine last night."

JD bypassed the washroom. Instead, he went straight to the side door of the convenience store. He looked out and saw Maggie. She raised her hand and waved at him. Out of the corner of his eye, he noticed a movement coming from the roadside of the parking lot.

It was a dishevelled man running at full speed. He slashed the air with what appeared to be a knife as he went. The man headed straight towards Maggie. JD held the door wide and shouted.

"Run, Maggie!"

Maggie looked at JD in confusion and then noticed the man rushing towards her. He was coming at a fast pace and getting close. He'd catch her if she didn't move fast. Her heart raced, and she ran towards JD. Her cowboy boots slipped out as she tried to gain traction on the smooth pavement. She cursed under her breath at her choice of boots instead of the running shoes she should have worn. Then her feet caught, and she propelled forward to JD and safety.

JD pulled the door closed as soon as she entered. He locked it as the man slammed into the glass. In his hand, he held a box cutter and was raving. JD placed an arm protective arm around Maggie's shoulders.

"Lock the front door!" JD called out to the young man, working the cash. He looked down at Maggie. "Are you ok?"

"I'm fine, thanks to you." Maggie wrapped her arms around his waist and squeezed him. JD just smiled.

The man banged on the glass. In his agitated state, he swore at them and spit at the window. People got back into their vehicles and locked the doors. Patrons from the restaurant, after hearing the commotion, came out to investigate.

"Call 911 before he hurts someone." A server called out.

"I'm on it." Replied the young man, who was working behind the cash in the store.

Josh joined Maggie and JD.

"What's going on?"

They filled him in on everything that had happened so far. They stayed there and continued to monitor the man as he approached cars at the fuel island and charged at the front doors, banging on them, demanding to be let in.

It wasn't long before the police arrived. The cops told him to drop his knife. He didn't. Instead, he continued to slice at the air with it. The cops got out of their vehicles with their guns drawn, shielded by the cruisers' open doors.

Soon a police van showed up, and out jumped an officer and K9 unit. Again, they told him to drop his weapon. When he still didn't comply, they released the K9. The dog raced towards the man and took him down, with its handler close behind.

It didn't take long before the dog had him on the ground and the officers were handcuffing him. They led him to the nearest cruiser; the weapon bagged as evidence, and the cops took him away.

"There's never a dull moment here." Josh joked as he unlocked the door. "I'm glad you're OK Maggie. Let's go get our breakfast ordered."

Maggie trembled as they made their way back to the table, JD's arm still wrapped around her shoulders. They weren't in a hurry, so they took their time eating their breakfast and discussed the mornings' excitement with other patrons nearby.

44

NOELLE

It was just before the supper hour when Noelle arrived at the Husky. Instead of finding most of the drivers in their cabs, she found herself surprised to find small groups of people standing around chatting. It didn't take long for her to discover what all the commotion was about. It was all anyone talked about, the man with the knife. She heard how he chased after Maggie and her narrow escape. Everyone was saying one of her fellow driver's, JD, was a hero. He saw what was happening and got her to safety. Noelle sighed. It would be nice to have someone care enough about her to protect her like that.

She knew who they were talking about. All the locals were familiar with Bob. He was a homeless man with mental health issues and his behaviours made him memorable. She also knew that the Husky staff often gave him food on the verge of expiring, instead of throwing it out, which was why he was always around. He still checked out the dumpster for empty bottles to turn in for cash if he didn't get the bags the driver's left on the ground.

She didn't know where he slept, nor did she care. But all this chatter was cramping her style. Until the drivers headed back to their rigs, no one wanted her company.

She stayed close to a group of truckers that once again retold the story. None of them had witnessed it firsthand, but that didn't stop them from embellishing the tale. They hadn't even been at the Husky when it happened, Noelle smiled at their need to be involved no matter what. By the time she'd heard the last trucker tell the tale, instead of the K9 unit taking Bob down, they used their tasers on him with guns blasting. Noelle rolled her eyes and went towards the building.

Noelle parked her bike and pulled out a cigarette. She figured one way to get their attention was to ask for a light. She approached one gathering of men.

"Hi. Anyone got a light?" She smiled, showing her cigarette poised between her index and middle fingers.

"Sure." One of the burlier men responded, pulling out a lighter, flicking it, and holding it up for her.

When she leaned in, she gave them all a glimpse of her cleavage. She had good boobs and wore bras that helped to lift them and show them off. Low-cut tops came in handy as well. But not too low; no need to give away too much for free. They didn't seem to mind her hanging around, so she added to the conversation by dropping bits of gossip she'd picked up along her route.

Before long, the burly man who lit her cigarette showed an interest in her. The signs were discrete, but there. Noelle excused herself so that he could approach her in private.

"It was nice talking to y'all. I've got to get moving." She said as she walked away, adding just enough sway to her slender hips as she went.

She got back on her bicycle and headed to the building and stretched her body, arms in the air, her breasts straining against the fabric of her t-shirt. A quick glance over her shoulder confirmed they were watching. She smiled to herself as she rode over to the dumpster to lock up her bike.

Just as she clicked the lock closed, she peered up to see the man approaching her. She smiled at him. He looked around to determine if anyone saw he was talking to her and asked if she'd meet him at his truck. He let her know which one it was and continue in his way. She waited just long enough for him to get situated before she joined him. Once again, another night of work had begun.

45

RYAN

*I*t took two days for the road crews to dig out of the mess from the snowstorm. They'd cleared the lot where he parked, but he still had to hand shovel the snow that was piled up away from his truck and trailer so he could get moving. His delivery was in two parts. The first was in Edmonton. If the roads stayed open, he would be there in about 11 hours. He'd deliver the rest of his load into Vancouver. It should take about 12 hours to make it to Vancouver from Edmonton. But he only planned to go as far as Chilliwack, so that he could deliver during business hours.

He needed to call Krissy and let her know his plan, so he picked up the phone.

"Hello." Her voice chimed over the line.

"I love you today."

"And I love you today." Ryan heard the smile in her voice when she responded to him.

"I wanted to let you know I'm back on the road, and I should get into Edmonton tonight."

"Just be careful. They may have cleared the roads, but I realize they will still be snow-covered and icy."

Ryan laughed. "Yes, Dear."

"Don't you, yes dear me!" She mocked, trying to sound stern.

"Ahh." Ryan chuckled. "I miss you, baby."

"Let me guess, with every bullet so far?" Krissy quipped.

Ryan couldn't help the laughter that burst from his lips. "I'm kidding, babe," she replied, "and I miss you, too."

"How are the kids?" He asked.

"Why don't you call them after school and ask them yourself? You know they love to talk to you. Jessica is getting annoyed with me when I tell you their news. Daniel has said nothing yet, but I know he agrees with her."

"News? They have news?" Ryan cut in.

"If they do, I can't tell you. You'll have to call when the kids get home."

"Ok, ok. I can take a hint. I'll call them later and they can tell me what's going on."

"Thanks, sweetie. They'll appreciate it."

"Well, I should go, especially since I'll be calling again later."

"Ok, baby, and Ryan, be careful out there. We love you."

"I always am, baby. I love you too."

Ryan sighed when he disconnected the call. There was so much he missed while driving the truck. But he was trucking when he met Krissy, and she knew what to expect. It bothered him knowing he missed the day-to-day events, but his family didn't know any difference. It was the life they'd always had. Phone calls helped. Ryan didn't know what he would have done before cell phones, and Krissy took videos of important events, but it wasn't the same. He thought about getting a local driving job. He wouldn't make the same money, but he'd be home every night. It was something he and Krissy could talk about it when he got home.

46

FRANK

*A*nger bubbled inside of him. He couldn't understand why the plows took so long to clear the roads. He pounded his fist on the steering wheel. Traffic was moving, but he'd ran out of snacks, and his pee bottle was full. He'd wait until there was less traffic and chuck it out the window. His milk jug was almost empty. He could use that if he needed to. One of the first things on his agenda was to stop and stock up on supplies. This time of year, you never knew when you'd get storm-stayed.

He didn't need to sniff his underarms to know he also required a shower. He knew he stunk. His truck needed fuel anyway, so he could kill two birds with the proverbial fuel stop. In hindsight, Frank regretted his rash decision to push through the storm. If he'd been thinking, he'd have stopped at a truck stop along the way where he'd have access to everything he needed.

Frank pulled off at the next truck stop to take care of everything, from fuel to shower. He dumped out his pee jug, choosing not to toss it on the roadside. Many younger drivers did, but he was old school and even though the thought crossed his mind, in the end he couldn't do it. He may not shower as often as he should, but he wouldn't litter the highway with piss jugs. If he did, with his luck, he'd end up getting caught by a ticket-happy officer and get delayed even more.

He didn't have any other options for toileting while he was stuck in a snowstorm. Under the circumstances, he had to improvise with what was available to him.

Now that he was clean and his supplies stocked up, he got back into his rig and headed west on Highway 1. He'd make it to his delivery on time and spend the night in Chilliwack while he waited for his return load.

As he made his way along the icy highway, he shook his head at how many trucks he saw in the ditches. He found several trucks still protruded from snowbanks, and some flipped on their sides. The highway looked like a trucker's boneyard. Frank noticed a few cars were also off the road, but only a handful. He could only assume that the truckers either miss read the road conditions or got cut off by a four-wheeler. It disgusted Frank at how many stupid, untrained truckers were on the road these days. The car drivers were also to blame for the carnage on the highway. They cut off truckers in a hurry to be first.

First to the scene of the accident,' he thought with disgust.

It may have stopped snowing, but the prairies' flat landscape offered no protection from the wind that kicked up. With each gust, swirls of snow caught and puffed over the highway, creating near whiteout conditions. Frank slowed down and put on his four ways. That way, anyone coming up his rear could see his lights, even if they couldn't see him. He hoped that when he got through the prairies, the roads would clear up. Of course, who knew what he'd encounter in the Rockies?

47

MAGGIE

$\mathcal{M}$aggie stepped out of the trailer to take a walk and stretch her legs. She'd had enough of sitting around drinking, rehashing what happened, and needed a break from it all. They'd eaten a nice BBQ dinner together, but the crowd was getting rowdy, and she needed a change of pace.

She walked up and down the rows of trucks. Then she spotted the truck of the guy she'd helped tie down the load in Sault Saint Marie. Maggie struggled to remember his name, and then it popped into her head. Ryan. His name was Ryan.

His truck was dark inside, but the curtains were open. He might still be inside. Maggie gave a quick rap on the door to check, but there was no answer. She decided if she found him, she'd invite him back for a drink. The road was lonely, and he might like some company, and that the group was mostly men would ease his wife's mind, she thought with a chuckle.

She continued on to the convenience store. A noise to her right startled her. She was still a little jumpy after this morning, and she turned her head. It was only someone out walking their dog, but in her distraction, she had almost bumped right into Ryan. He had his head down, looking at his phone, and he mumbled an apology without looking at her.

"Ryan? It's me, Maggie. We met in Sault Saint Marie."

He lifted his head and broke into a smile. Not that he had to lift it far. He was well over six feet and she was just a little bitty thing.

"Maggie! Well, fancy meeting you here!" A smile stretched from ear to ear.

"I've been here a few days. I'm on a car tour and I'm waiting to pick up in Vancouver. Hey, there's a bunch of us gathered in my trailer. Do you feel like coming back to hang out?"

Ryan hesitated. Maggie sensed he was uncomfortable with the idea, so she continued. "There are half a dozen car haulers sitting in my trailer right now. I just needed a break, so I took a walk. Why don't you come by and see? If it's not your scene, just say hi?"

She could see him mull it over before he responded. "Sure, that sounds great! I have to call my family first. Which one is yours again?"

"Big Red, remember? We're all parked together in the rear row, far left side. Mine is the one in the middle. The drivers from Totter are there too. When you're finished talking to your family, just come on over."

"Are you sure it will be alright?" He questioned as he glanced to the back row and all the enclosed vehicle trucks.

"My trailer, my rules. Of course, it's ok. We just finished eating, but there are a ton of leftovers. Come and have some. No reason to stay up here by yourself unless you want to."

"Ok, I can always eat, thank you. I'll be there in a few minutes."

"I'll go tell the guys to expect you. It won't take long to turn the BBQ back on and warm some of the food."

Ryan smiled at her. "Thanks, you're one of a kind."

Maggie left Ryan in his truck and made her way back to her trailer. She realized JD would tease her. He said she was always picking up strays.

MAGGIE CLIMBED BACK UP into the trailer, but not before she started the BBQ. JD smelled the BBQ going and turned to Maggie as she stepped up inside.

"Well, that's a fine how-do-ya-do. I thought you had enough to eat, Mags."

She chuckled. "It's not for me."

"Let me guess, you've found a stray." JD teased. Maggie rolled her eyes. JD was predictable. But he was genuine, so she smiled at him.

"No, this time it's not a stray, it's a friend." She replied as she sat down. "I ran into him in Sault Saint Marie. He's a flat decker, and his tarp got caught in the wind, so I climbed onto his trailer and gave him a hand."

"Of course you did, Maggie." Josh cut in. "You know there's someone out there killing truckers. How can you be sure it's not him?"

Maggie laughed and retorted. "How do you know it's not me?"

With that, everyone broke into peals of laughter. Tammy snorted so hard beer came out of her nose and she fell out of her chair, which caused a fresh round of laughter.

"Ok, all kidding aside. Ryan's a nice guy. He's giving his family a call, and then he's going to join us. I told him we had lots of leftovers, and I offered to warm some up for him. So be nice!"

"Ok, Maggie, we'll be nice. We were only teasing you." JD interjected.

The group fell back into regular conversation while they waited for Ryan to join them. JD even slipped over to his trailer to grab another chair.

4 8

NOELLE

$\mathcal{N}$oelle rolled over in her bed and stretched. Today was laundry day. First, she'd hop in the shower so she could add her towel to the basket, then she'd strip the sheets from her bed before gathering up the rest of her dirty clothes.

She slipped her feet into her slippers and counted out the money she earned this week. It had been a good work week. She had plenty of money. Maybe she'd take the night off. She debated on whether to take a walk or just stay in when she finished her laundry. One thing she needed to do was clean her apartment. It was small, so it wouldn't take her long.

She stepped out of the shower and rubbed her body dry with her favourite towel before tossing it into the hamper. Then Noelle took the time to rub moisturizer onto her skin before spraying some mousse in her hands and running it through her damp hair, spiking the ends.

She peered into the mirror and decided not to put on any make-up. She wouldn't be trying to impress anyone today. Noelle pulled on a pair of yoga pants and an old t-shirt before gathering the laundry supplies and heading down to the laundry room.

She filled two washing machines and put the coins in the slot to start the loads. She had about 45 minutes before the wash ended, and she'd need to transfer it to the dryer, so she'd just run upstairs and start cleaning her place. With any luck, by the time she finished her laundry, her apartment would be clean.

NOELLE PLOPPED down on her sofa and surveyed the room. She lifted her chin with a sense of pride at a job well done. With her apartment clean and her laundry folded and put away, she decided it was a good time to run some errands. She'd leave her bicycle on her balcony. Noelle associated her bike with work, preferring to walk when she was on her off time. She slung a backpack over her shoulder to carry her groceries. She never bought more food than she needed to last her a couple of days.

Her first stop was the Safeway for some staples, and on impulse, threw in a bag of sour cream and onion potato chips. She didn't eat chips often, but thought she'd stream a movie later, and it would be nice to have something to munch on while she watched. Her last stop was the butcher. Noelle wanted a couple of their chili mango chicken breasts. She'd cook them both up tonight and eat the second one tomorrow with a salad.

She walked past the Husky on her way home and looked at the rows of trucks. Noelle noticed that the car haulers were still in the back row. She wondered how much longer they planned to stick around and hoped they would leave soon. Her biggest concern today was making sure no one else was working her territory. Noelle may not be working today, but she didn't want anyone else to work the lot, either. She couldn't see anyone else there, and she breathed a sigh of relief.

She'd vowed to herself to show up earlier tomorrow. Noelle expected a few of her regulars to arrive and knew she'd be busy. But tonight was all hers.

She climbed the three flights of stairs to her unit and went inside, dropping her backpack on the counter before heading to the washroom to relieve herself. Noelle slipped out of her clothes and into a ratty oversized t-shirt, put the groceries away before settling on the couch to watch TV, forgetting about the truck stop and her work.

49

RYAN

*A*fter he ran into Maggie, Ryan headed back to his truck to call Krissy. He climbed up in and settled onto his seat before keying in the number.

"Hey, baby." She breathed into the phone as she answered.

"Hi, sweetie. I'm parked in Chilliwack for the night."

"Oh, that's good. Do you have your reloads yet?" Krissy asked.

"No. They'll let me know in the morning."

"Mmm, ok."

"Did I catch you at a bad time?" Ryan asked.

"Sorry, baby, I was just looking over Jessica's homework. I'll put it down and look at it when we get off the phone. You have my full attention."

Ryan chuckled. "Do you remember me telling you about the female trucker who helped me with my tarp that day?"

"Um, yes, her name's Maggie, right?"

"Yes. Well, Maggie and her friends invited me to join them for a drink. They also have leftover BBQ for me. Would it upset you if I went?"

Krissy's soft laughter drifted across the line.

"Sweetheart, of course, it wouldn't bother me. I know you spend too much time alone and that your brothers and sisters on the road are your extended family."

Ryan sighed. He knew what she'd say before he asked, but he kept nothing from her. The secret to their happy marriage was considering, 'What would my partner think?' before doing something. Over the years, it worked well. If it bothered her, there was no way he'd go. He'd just set up his TV, pop a meal in the microwave, and put in a movie.

"You're the best baby."

"The best you're going to get." She quipped back.

"Alright," he smiled, "well, I'm heading over there now. I'm three hours behind you, so you'll be in bed when I return. I'll say good night now. I love you and the kids. Sleep well."

"We love you too. Have fun." With that, he disconnected the line. Ryan looked at his phone, and his chest swelled with pride. Daniel said he got an 'A' on his math test and Jessica said she had a lead in the school play. He knew he had an amazing wife and that he was a lucky guy.

RYAN LOCKED his truck and made his way to the back row, where Maggie and her friends were. As he approached, the tantalizing aroma of barbecue filled his nostrils, and his stomach grumbled. It surprised him how hungry he was and felt blessed that they'd offered to share. He could hear the animated conversation coming from within the trailer. He noticed that the side door was wide open, so he peered in.

Silence fell as all faces turned his way. There was an awkwardness, and he hesitated before stepping inside. He relaxed when Maggie popped out of her seat to greet him.

"RYAN! Come on in and meet everyone, and I'll grab you a plate of food."

She made the round of introductions and handed him a heaping plate of food. The awkwardness he felt at first didn't take long to disappear and soon they were all talking like old friends, sharing stories from on the road.

Ryan wasn't sure why, but he shared the story about what he discovered as a new driver twenty years ago, the one that almost forced him to give up trucking. He told them about the father and daughter he found. He couldn't help himself from getting choked up as he spoke. Ryan always wondered what happened to the child. He knew the father had died at the scene, but the last time he saw the child, she was being whisked away in an ambulance. The experience changed his outlook, and he vowed to be a better man because of it. When he finished, he noticed the look of shock on most of the faces, but it was the tears in Maggie's eyes that tore at his heart and he regretted saying anything to upset her.

The mood remained sombre until JD told everyone about one of his crazy adventures. Soon they were all laughing again, but Ryan still felt terrible that his story upset Maggie. Every so often throughout the evening, he looked up at her and several times caught her looking at him with a strange look on her face.

50

FRANK

*D*arkness had fallen when he pulled into the Husky in Chilliwack. The parking lot was full, but he moved close to the last truck in the second row, creating a spot for himself. He checked his mirror and felt satisfied that others could get around him and as long as no one else parked beside him, everything would be fine. It would be tight, but possible.

He turned off his truck and climbed out for a pee. As he did, he noticed the commotion taking place from the car haulers behind him. Frank grumbled under his breath. He was beat, and if they didn't shut up soon, he would shut them up.

Frank scowled as he looked towards the row of trucks and saw the light coming from inside a trailer. He clenched his fist and walked over to say something to them, when what he assumed was the local lot lizard approached him. She pulled her bicycle up beside him and smiled.

"Are you looking for some company?" She purred.

He looked her up and down. She was attractive enough, but she had a hard edge to her. He preferred them younger and sweeter, or at least girls who appeared to be. He supposed if he just got a blow job, he could close his eyes and pretend she was someone else.

"How much for a blow job?" Frank barked at her.

He watched as she swivelled her head around to check if anyone heard him. Frank's eyes narrowed. Discretion might be required. He assumed she only got away with working the lots by not being obvious. He was about to tell her to forget it when she spoke.

"Why don't we discuss that in your truck? If we can't agree on terms, I'll leave. No questions asked."

Frank gave her the once over and decided that she was small enough, but the black hair and eyeliner made her look tough. But he thought with his eyes closed, it wouldn't matter. In the end, he agreed because he needed the release.

He climbed up into his rig and unlocked the door for her to join him and discuss the money. Noelle asked for half up front. Frank had no problem paying her as long as she satisfied him and left the other half on the dashboard. When they finished, she could take the rest of her money and go.

WHEN THE HOOKER LEFT, Frank laid back on his bunk. She'd been a release, but he didn't feel satisfied. He stroked his beard and decided it was time to locate someone more to his liking. When he did, it left him sated for months. It had been a long time since he fulfilled his desires, but his tastes were particular, and it wasn't easy to find someone who fit the bill. He kept his eyes and his options open wherever he went because he never knew when the opportunity would present itself.

Frank reached under his bunk and pulled out his ribbon of souvenirs and clipped them back to the roof of his cab.

HE'D GOT in first to pull them down before the working girl got into his truck. She didn't need to see them. He was proud of them, but he didn't want some nosey bitch asking questions.

With the ribbon hanging back up within sight, he relaxed, turned off the lights to his cab, and drifted off to sleep.

51

DR. COLEMAN

*A*udrey settled down on her sofa. The call she had from 156 this afternoon left her nerves raw. An icy chill crept into her bones, and she made a fire. She needed something, anything, to keep from remembering the past. Her own pain and sorrow drifted to the surface, no matter how hard she tried to bottle it up.

When the fire was roaring, she padded to the kitchen to pour herself a gin and tonic. She debated whether to bring the bottle and ice bucket back to the living room, but decided against it. Having it close at hand would make it too easy to overindulge. What she relished was the numbing effects of the alcohol, which allowed her to push her memories aside, the ones she wished she could forget.

WHILE ENJOYING her second glass of G & T, she couldn't prevent her memories from filtering back to the horror of the events that happened more years ago than she cared to remember. Before that, happiness filled her life.

Her daughter's joy and innocence were beautiful, and she was so full of life. In those days, times had been simpler. Or so she and her husband thought. Predators didn't lurk around every corner and you didn't have to worry so much about strangers. As long as you monitored your child, everything was fine. But that was a lie.

Her daughter Sara and husband Rick had a daddy/daughter day. She'd let them go without thinking; she was feeling overwhelmed with work and motherhood. When Rick suggested she take a little time for herself, she jumped at it. She didn't know that the decision she made that day would take everything from her. How could she?

From what she was told, Sara and Rick stopped at a restaurant along the highway on their way home while she sat curled up with a book at home. After they ate, Rick had to use the washroom, and he left Sara at the table. He thought she'd be okay in a crowded restaurant. Nothing would happen. Or so he thought.

When he returned, Sara was nowhere to be found. He called out for her, looked under the tables, had the server check in the washroom for her. She'd vanished. Nobody saw her leave; no one saw who took her. They notified the police and Rick made the anguished call to Audrey, who raced to the roadside restaurant to help search for Sara.

When she arrived, the police had searched through parked cars and dumpsters. Audrey broke down when she learned the police searched the dumpsters in the area. The thought that someone may have disposed of her daughter like trash was more than she could bear. When Rick came to her, his face was ashen and tear-streaked. She collapsed into his arms, and they both cried. The search continued, but they didn't find her, not then, anyway.

They stayed in a nearby hotel and went out daily with volunteers searching the area for Sara. Hundreds of people walked along the roadside and through fields calling their child's name. When they returned on that last day, she saw their faces; the grave looks in their eyes. She knew everyone thought her daughter was dead. In her heart, Audrey knew Sara was already dead. But she couldn't admit it, even to herself. After a few days, the police told them to go home. They said they'd contact them if there were any new leads, but the only information she expected was that they'd found her daughter's body.

After Sara's disappearance, Rick wasn't the same. They stopped communicating with each other unless it was about the search. Every morning, Audrey drove up to that restaurant and looked for Sara. Guilt overcame her for wanting a day to herself. She felt if she hadn't, Sara would be with them and fine. Suffering with her own grief, she overlooked Rick's.

Although Rick continued to work, he wasn't eating and drank too much. As time went on, they argued all the time. She blamed him for taking his eyes off Sara, and he blamed Audrey for needing some alone time.

Then they got the call no parent wanted to get. They'd found Sara's body. The police got a tip and discovered her in an abandoned warehouse near to the restaurant. The evidence determined the killer had assaulted her prior to being strangled. Because whoever did it got away without a trace, they suggested the possibility that he was a truck driver or traveller who stopped at the restaurant. The restaurant was part of the truck stop, so truckers frequented it, and it was right off the highway. They found all of Sara's belongings with her body, except one of the two yellow plastic hair clips she had in her hair emblazoned with her name.

When the call came, Rick walked out. Audrey crumbled to the sofa, sobbing for her child. She needed Rick; they needed to grieve together, and they had to identify their only child's body and plan a funeral. Soon her sorrow turned to anger, anger that someone had taken her only child and anger that her husband left her to deal with everything on her own.

She was alone when she arrived to identify her battered child's body. She peered through the window as the coroner pulled back the sheet. The swollen, bruised face of her daughter was almost unrecognizable. Audrey also saw the bruises on her neck, the bruises that marked how Sara's killer had squeezed the life out of her. Her precious daughter, used and discarded like trash. The officer beside her supported her as she sagged under the stress. He walked her to a small room, offered her a seat, and got her a glass of water. Audrey grabbed a tissue from the box on the table, and she allowed the tears to balloon in her eyes before popping and running down her cheeks.

The sobs echoed in the tiny room. The officer tried to console her until he got called from the room.

When he returned, his face was grave. A well-dressed woman followed him in, her heels clipped on the worn linoleum. Audrey's water filled eyes looked up as they entered and wondered what else they had to say to add to her grief. Then the officer spoke.

"I'm sorry, Mrs. Coleman. Under the circumstances, I wish I didn't have to tell you this. But word just came in."

Audrey waited, her chest tightening, certain they were going to tell her more about what happened to Sara.

"We were just notified that your husband was killed in an accident," he replied softly.

Silence filled the air with a smothering gloom that choked the small space. Audrey's jaw sagged and her hands dropped into her lap. She shook her head. No, there was no way she heard him correctly.

"You're lying!" She shouted, her fists balling up, tearing at the tissue in her hand. "There is no way my husband is dead!"

"I'm sorry. They have identified him. There's no mistake."

"What? How? When? No, you're mistaken." Audrey fired at him.

"His office found a suicide note for you, and he went to the roof of his office tower and jumped. I'm very sorry. This is Dr. Paranã. She's a clinical grief therapist. She's here to help."

Audrey didn't hear the rest of what the officer told her. In her head, she screamed at Rick. *You coward! This was your fault! Now you've left me to deal with everything!* Before she collapsed to the floor.

When she was stable enough to deal with Rick and Sara's deaths, she took their bodies back to the town she grew up in and buried them there. It was difficult, but she'd forgiven Rick long ago. He didn't have the strength she did, and his guilt ate away at him until he broke. The confirmation that Sara was dead and what had happened to her finished him.

Audrey grew from the experience and devoted her life to helping others. Whether it was to overcome grief, trauma, or just an ear, she listened to her clients and helped them through their difficulties. The only client she'd ever told the story to was 156, and that was because she thought it would help.

5 2

CHILLIWACK, B.C.

*N*o one lurked in the deserted parking lot. No one except two, the hunter and the hunted. Traffic still sped past on the road, but most of the trucks were dark as their drivers slept. The hunter was restless and wandered the lot.

That's when it happened. The hunter noticed a glow coming from the cab of a truck and observed the man inside, who was looking at pictures on his tablet. Photos he wouldn't want to be seen by anyone, photos that shouldn't exist, but did. The man was oblivious to what lay ahead because someone else saw those quick, fleeting images that flicked across his screen as he scrolled. Someone who felt the rage simmer beneath the surface. The uncontrollable, all-consuming rage.

The images on his screen depicted the man's actual perversions. These images he looked at when he thought he was alone. The ones he'd get arrested for if anyone found them. He thought he'd been able to hide his true self, but he was wrong. His stalker saw the pictures no matter how fleeting and recognized what he was.

The man turned off his tablet and slipped out of his truck. Eyes watching from the shadows never left him as he shuffled up to the building, tossed his garbage and returned.

The hunter glanced around as the prey returned to his truck. The parking lot was well lit, the lines of rigs created the only shadows. Darkness was better for killing. But this man had to die. It had to be now. Allowing this perverted man to continue down the road was a threat to children. Finding him again would take too long. The world wouldn't miss him.

Quiet steps allowed the killer to sneak up on the man as he climbed back into his truck. A hand reached out and pulled him back. He stumbled off the stairs and turned to face the person who grabbed him. His jaw slackened and his eyes widened in surprise. Before he could say anything, the knife slid across his throat. Blood spurted outward, coating the reversed raincoat in crimson gore as the man crumbled into a heap.

The killer's chest heaved with long breaths to create a calmness. Slow, deliberate movements were used to remove the blood-splattered coat and gloves before balling them up for disposal. Next, the blood needed to be washed from the knife to be used another time. The last step was to toss the small pink plastic hair clip to the ground beside the body, watching as it landed in the pool of blood.

Unable to leave the truck stop, this time the killer poured lighter fluid over the bag of soiled plastic garments and lit it on fire. The flames would destroy the evidence. Only a melted blob of plastic would remain. When the flames had extinguished themselves, the killer kicked the melted mess under the dumpster, and hoped no one would find it.

The hunter continued to the washrooms, face hidden beneath a ball cap, knife hidden up a sleeve. The clerk didn't even bother to look up. Some soap and water would clean off the knife, and remove the aroma of lighter fuel. Some wipes would take care of any blood spots that may have landed where the plastic didn't cover.

Clean and with a new sense of purpose, the killer sprinted along the perimeter, back to the rig to sleep. The crime was undetected, and the body remained undiscovered. A deep sigh escaped into the pillow as sleep came.

53

RYAN

Ryan left the shower stall just as a tiny French man ran into the Husky convenience store, his hands covered in blood. He stopped dead in his tracks, his eyes wide as the man screamed in a mixture of French and broken English. The only words he understood were 'call 911'.

The girl working behind the counter stepped back from him before she picked up the phone. Her hands trembled as she made the call. Ryan walked up to the front to see if he could help. The man wrung his hands as he headed to the washroom to clean up. Ryan followed and stopped him.

"Hey buddy, you'd better not wash the blood off. When the cops get here, they'll ask questions, and we saw the blood on you. If you wash it off, it will be suspicious."

"Oh, mon Dieu. Je vous remercie." The man replied. On noting the confused expression on Ryan's face, he realized Ryan didn't understand him. So, he muttered, "Tanks."

The man, visibly shaken, clenched his hands as he waited for the police. Ryan wanted to head back to his truck, but thought he'd better stick around. He witnessed the French man enter the building, his hands covered in blood, and knew the police would want to speak to him. He didn't know what happened, but knew it wasn't good.

It wasn't long before the sound of sirens broke the early morning silence with a whir and a scream, blue lights flashing as the first cruiser screeched to a halt by the front of the doors. Ryan eyed the French man who paced about the store with nervous energy. Soon, two officers entered the store and spoke to the cashier. She told them what she knew and pointed to the man covered in blood. One officer asked Ryan a few questions, then told him to stay nearby in case they needed to question him again, as the other officer followed the French man out to the crime scene.

Ryan gave the officer his contact information and the details to which rig was his before he left the store. He went straight to his truck and put away his gear. The police officer was right behind him to join up with the other officer. A flashlight scanned the pavement, revealing a body. Ryan's steps faltered as his mind struggled with the image before him.

Ryan couldn't believe what he saw! Another victim of murder. He hoped the victim wasn't one of the driver's he'd spent the last couple of days with. Ryan especially hoped it wasn't Maggie. He couldn't tell whether the body was male or female. He liked her a lot and found her spunk and tenacity refreshing.

Ryan arrived back at the scene just as the officers covered the body. He breathed a sigh of relief after he glimpsed the bloody corpse and was sure it wasn't anyone he knew. He stepped back into the gathering crowd to watch. Ryan felt sorry for the French man. Of the two trucks that had caution tape surrounding them, one belonged to him. He assumed the other belonged to the victim.

It didn't take long for him to notice the cops had barricaded the entrances and exits to the parking lot. It looked like he wasn't going to be leaving soon. He gazed up at the overcast sky, streaked with glimmering light as the sun struggled to peek through. He had to call to his dispatch and tell them what happened. This time he was lucky it wasn't him who found the body, but it didn't matter, he was still a witness of sorts. He moved away from the crowd to make the call.

AFTER TAKING CARE OF EVERYTHING, except calling Krissy, he made his way back to the gathering crowd around the crime scene. He recognized JD's cowboy hat in the group and walked towards him, knowing that the car haulers would all be together and he could check on Maggie's safety. He perceived a strange protectiveness for her, something he didn't understand. It was almost fatherly.

The group of car haulers stood around chatting about what they learned, guessing about how long the cops would detain them, and what happened. Ryan filled them in on what he knew. Soon, they headed into the restaurant to have breakfast.

When they finished eating and were on their way out, Ryan saw Maggie bump into another driver and her violent reaction to the incident shocked him. He didn't understand what happened or what set her off and stood by, feeling overwhelmed by helplessness as she cried into JD's shoulder. Ryan knew there was a story there, but he wouldn't pry.

When Maggie had cried out, she brushed away her tears and apologized before leading the group to the back row. He noticed the set of her shoulders and thought how strong she was. Ryan had some calls to make, so he excused himself. He needed to give Krissy a call and tell her what happened, but promised to join them when he finished.

54

MAGGIE

The sound of sirens startled Maggie awake. She rubbed the sleep from her eyes to the sound of someone banging on the side of her cab.

"Maggie! Are you in there? Are you alright?" Josh called out. He sounded frantic.

She slipped into a pair of jeans and a sweatshirt before she opened the door.

"Oh, my god! You're ok. They won't let anyone over there, and we found out someone discovered a body. We got worried when we didn't see you."

Maggie's eyes widened before she responded. "A body? Where? Who?"

"Up in the first row. Nobody's saying anything. I don't even know who found it. We didn't see you and got worried."

Maggie smiled. "I guess I had more than I thought last night."

"For a minute there, we thought it was you! You don't normally sleep this late. I'm glad you're ok. Let's get closer and see what we can find out." JD suggested, as he stepped up beside Josh.

As they made their way closer to where the emergency vehicles were, Maggie saw the yellow police tape had marked off two trucks and trailers in the middle of the row. She shook her head. Why the guys thought she was the victim this far from her truck was beyond her.

"Oh crap! I hope he didn't suffer." Maggie swivelled her head as she tried to peer through the gathering crowd at the tarp-covered body still on the ground.

Just as it was out of her mouth, Ryan walked up and responded to her.

"The guy on the ground belongs to the blue Cascadia. The guy from the Volvo next to him found him earlier this morning."

Maggie patted his arm. "I'm glad you're ok Ryan."

He nodded in response.

"How did you find out?" Josh interjected.

"I was coming out of a shower early this morning when this guy ran into the store. There was blood on his hands, and he was hysterical. The girl working the cash called 911."

"Holy shit!" JD exclaimed. "That's a fine how-do-ya-do!" As he lifted his straw cowboy hat from his eyes and looked at the man talking to the police.

"Ya," Ryan replied, giving JD an odd look. "They aren't letting anyone leave the lot or come in. The cops have blocked off all the entrances and exits. I hear they're waiting for some detective from the RCMP to get here. I guess they'll want to talk to anyone who parked here last night from what the cop said. They'll be looking for witnesses. I've already contacted my dispatch and told them I was going to be held up. I can't believe I'm being held up at another crime scene."

Maggie's eyebrows drew together as she looked up at Ryan. She realized he'd been hoping to get a load out today and head back home to his family, and she felt bad that he was being delayed.

"I'm sorry you're stuck here. At least we were already planning on another day or two. If you can't get out before morning, come eat with us again tonight."

"Thanks, Maggie. I'm hoping I'll get to meet with the detectives soon, then I can get moving. The detective they're waiting for was close by, I heard. I think he's investigating the serial killer. Rumour has it they think this is his work."

Josh looked at Maggie and noticed her eyes widen before he spoke.

"Mags, I think from now on we should stay in pairs. This creep may still be nearby."

Chuckling, Maggie replied, "Yes, Dad." Josh rewarded her comment with a scowl.

"Seeing as we can't do much else, why don't we go inside for breakfast? If you haven't eaten, Ryan, why don't you join us?" JD asked, as he slung a protective arm around Maggie's shoulder. "I don't have a problem sticking close to Maggie." She rewarded him with a playful punch in the ribs.

"Sounds good to me. I'm starving. I'll call Krissy after we eat. The less time she knows about this, the better. All she'll do is worry."

Josh grinned from ear to ear. "I hear ya, buddy. Little momma is the same."

They slipped inside to eat and waste time while they waited for the detective to arrive. They enjoyed a filling, hot breakfast as crowds formed along the sidewalk. Just as Ryan said, officers had blocked the entrance to the parking lot. No one could leave before being questioned. The whole restaurant was chatting about what happened, with all kinds of speculations who the killer was.

Needing to make room for the growing line of customers, they left. As they left the building, Maggie bumped into an unkempt trucker with a long grey beard. Without looking up, she mumbled an apology. He stood in front of her, looked her up and down, noting her tiny youthful frame before his face split into a grin.

"No worries, little lady." He rasped as he moved aside.

A shiver ran down her spine at the sound of his voice. Her face went ashen as her stomach lurched. Her tongue stuck to the roof of her mouth. In her haste, she nodded at him before she pushed ahead of her companions and rushed out the door. It wasn't until she was outside in the glaring sunshine that she stopped. Bent over, with her hands on her knees, she tried to calm her racing heart. A hand reached out and touched her shoulder.

Her immediate response was violent. She lashed out, her arm striking out in defence, not seeing the concerned, friendly faces of her companions, until JD wrapped his arms around her and held her tight in a bear hug until she stopped flailing. Her chest heaved as she pulled air into her lungs to calm herself before turning and sobbing into JD's chest.

The three men exchanged glances at Maggie's reaction, but didn't comment. They couldn't understand her behaviour or what set her off. JD continued to hold her until she stopped crying. When Maggie pulled herself together, she pushed back from JD, but he still held onto her shoulders, his eyes searching hers. She muttered an apology, but it was obvious she wouldn't talk about what happened. Instead, she followed them back to the last row, where they'd parked their trucks and climbed inside hers, allowing herself time to think, leaving the men alone with their own thoughts.

55

NOELLE

F rom inside her apartment, Noelle heard the sirens and commotion coming from the Husky Truck Stop. She threw back her covers and sprinted onto her balcony wearing only an oversized t-shirt. She leaned over to get a better look.

There were cruisers blocking the entrances while they put up barricades along the sidewalk surrounding the Husky. Even from this distance, she made out the yellow tarp-covered body. She shuddered when she noticed how close it was to the last truck she was in the night before.

"Damn." She cursed as her cell phone rang, not bothering to look at the caller ID.

"Hello?"

"Noelle?"

"Yes. Who's this?"

"It's Candace. I heard they found a body at the Husky. You work in the area. So, I wanted to make sure you're ok."

"Thanks, Candace. Yes, I'm fine. I was out on my balcony watching all the excitement." Noelle walked back inside to grab her package of cigarettes and made herself a coffee. "Have you seen what's going on?"

"Well, I learned a bit about what happened. You're aware that my brother's dating one of the cash girls in the store. Well, anyway, she's working this morning. This guy came in bright and early, covered in blood, screaming about a body. Now they've shut the place down. I heard no one can leave or enter until some hot shot cop shows up."

Noelle hesitated for a minute and considered the information Candace told her. By the looks of things, it didn't appear as if she'd be working tonight, but if anyone told the cops that she worked the lot last night, they'd call her in for questioning. 'God dammit,' she thought. 'This complicates things.'

"I suppose I'd better stay away for now. No need to bring the fuzz to my door." Noelle responded.

"Sorry, Noelle, that won't fly. The cops will come looking for you; everyone knows you work the Husky. I'd suggest going there and hanging out in the restaurant. It will go better for you if you seem willing to talk."

Noelle lit her cigarette and took a long pull before blowing out a cloud of smoke. She didn't have a choice. Lots of people saw her there last night.

"Fuck! I guess you're right, Candace. Thanks for calling and checking on me. I'll shower and head over."

When she hung up the phone, she stubbed out her cigarette and finished the last sip of her coffee. She'd shower and go to the Husky before the cops started looking for her. She needed to decide if she should go in her full working girl regalia or tone it down a bit. Everyone there knew what she did for a living so the cops would too, but rubbing their faces in it would make trouble for herself.

In the end, she opted for a softer look. Even choosing to let her natural curls in her hair soften her appearance instead of going with her usual spikes. She grabbed some cash and slipped it into her tattered bag before tossing in her smokes. She wouldn't earn a dime today, but she was alive.

It was best to leave her bicycle behind. She didn't have a need for it. She wouldn't be riding around trying to entice business, and she couldn't afford to leave it unattended for too long.

Noelle set off to the Husky in a short jean skirt, tennis shoes, and a tank top. It was the only thing she owned that was appropriate attire. At least the weather was sunny and warm.

56

FRANK

The sound of blaring sirens dragged Frank from a deep sleep. He grumbled as he rolled over in his bunk. His bladder was on fire with the need to pee.

"What the fuck? Can't a fella get a peaceful night's sleep anymore?" He muttered as he scratched his belly before donning yesterday's clothing.

Frank climbed out of his cab to pee between the cab and the trailer until he realized that the commotion was in the parking lot and there were too many people hanging around. He'd be better off to take his wallet and head inside. He'd pee and grab something to eat. If he was lucky, things would settle down before he was done.

As he walked across the parking lot, he noticed the barricades blocking the exits. "Shit," he cursed out loud. "If the cops didn't get this mess figured out soon, I'll be late for my delivery." Frank planned to head straight to the building to use the washroom. Then he saw the crowd standing behind the yellow tape around the two trailers and made his way over. He stood back and listened. It was the best way to find out what was going on. Everyone was talking, so it didn't take him long to learn what happened. He hoped someone would know how long they planned to keep them here.

He stood behind a group of men who were talking and making raunchy jokes. Frank could just make out the yellow tarp from his vantage point, which he gathered was a body. He didn't engage with anyone, just listened in to discover what happened.

"How long are we going to be stuck here?" He heard one man ask.

"I believe they're waiting for some big shot RCMP detective. One cop said they think it's the work of that serial killer everyone's been blarin' about on the CB," responded another.

"Really? Holy fuck! It kinda hits home when you're at the same truck stop. I heard the chatter on the CB but thought little about it. I mean, I've never been at a truck stop when it happened before."

"From what I heard, a guy from Quebec in the truck next to him found the body. Can't imagine having to see that before my morning squirt." Laughter ran out from amongst the men as they continued talking.

Frank moved away from the group. All he was getting from them now was gossip and speculation. Frank learned what he needed and knew he wasn't going anywhere until the RCMP detective arrived and cleared the scene. His stomach growled, so he continued up to the main building to use the washroom and get something to eat while he waited.

As he entered the restaurant, and by accident, he bumped into a petite woman. She mumbled an apology without looking up. He looked her up and down. He noted her tiny, youthful frame and his face split into a grin.

"No worries, little lady." He rasped.

He saw her eyes widen, and she raced out of the restaurant. The guys with her stood in shock, but soon followed. Frank paused before he shook his head and continued inside.

57

MAGGIE

She told her companions she'd be right back, but she knew she needed more than a minute. Maggie climbed up into her rig. She had to calm herself. She wasn't sure why that man's voice caused her to react the way she did. It fuelled a long-buried memory that threatened to bubble up. She grabbed a cigarette, rolled down her window, and lit it. Took a deep, calming drag, and allowed the smoke to fill her lungs, and exhaled.

She glanced over at JD and Josh, who stood in front of JD's truck talking as Ryan returned to his rig to phone his wife. She saw them looking up and figured they were talking about her. Maggie didn't care what they thought and allowed the fist she'd clenched to unfurl. There was someone she should call, but thought better of it. Now wasn't the time. Instead, she finished her smoke and called out to the boys that she was making a pot of coffee for them, JD style.

On hearing this, a smile spread across JD's face; Josh smirked. Josh pulled out the folding chairs out of the trailer and set them up outside in the sunshine so they could enjoy their coffees. Neither of them would ask Maggie what happened. They knew if she wanted to talk, she would, so they'd just drop it.

Soon, Maggie left her truck carrying three steaming cups of

189

coffee. She'd added some Jack and French Vanilla to them to make them JD style. Maggie handed them each a cup and settled into her seat. She sipped on hers, allowing the warmth of the coffee and the jolt of Jack to warm her insides. The combination aided in calming her nerves.

"Did Ryan say when he'll be back to join us?" Maggie asked, motioning to the empty chair the boys set out for him.

"He's just calling his wife. He shouldn't be long. Why?" Josh responded.

"I figured I'd go for a walk and get something for supper. I want to hit Fraser Valley meats, maybe buy some more of those pork medallions for the BBQ. Plus, we need veggies, and I need another box of wine." Maggie laughed.

"I'll go with you," JD interjected. "With everything that's going on, I don't think you should be alone."

"Are you serious? The parking lot's full of cops. I assume I'll be safe. I want to take a walk and clear my head. When it's night, I'll let you be a gentleman and walk me to the loo." She finished with a smile.

JD gave her a smirk. "Fine, but when it gets dark, you're stuck with us. Deal?" He reached out a hand to shake on.

Maggie took his outstretched hand and shook it. "Deal!"

When they finished their coffees, Maggie placed the cups in the plastic tote in the trailer used to wash the dishes. The cups could wait until they had more to clean. There was no reason to boil water for just three dirty cups. Ryan still hadn't returned, so Maggie grabbed her bundle buggy and headed out. The first stop, BC Liquors. The heavy box of wine needed to be at the bottom of the buggy.

She left the parking lot by the sidewalk instead of cutting through it, as was her routine. She expected someone to stop her, knowing the cops wanted to talk to everyone parked there, but nobody did.

As she turned onto Vedder Road, she saw Noelle in the distance, heading towards her. She wondered if she should warn Noelle to stay away. With the parking lot full of cops, she couldn't work. Then she noticed Noelle wasn't wearing her work clothes, nor riding her bike. She was smart, and she wasn't heading to work. She must want to know what happened.

Maggie nodded at her as their paths crossed, and she continued on to get what they needed for dinner and clear her head. Her mind drifted back to the man with the raspy voice, and she shuddered. Her guts clenched, and she knew she'd have to find him when she returned and look for the telltale signs that would confirm her suspicions.

58

NOELLE

$\mathcal{N}$oelle took her time as she made her way to the Husky. Just ahead, she saw Maggie approaching, dragging her bundle buggy. Noelle wasn't sure why she got nervous when she ran into Maggie. But she did. When they passed each other, they just nodded. Noelle chuckled. It was comical when she thought about it, how they acknowledged each other, but didn't speak. *'Maggie wasn't rude to her, like some of the other female truck drivers.'* Noelle thought. *'But then again, she didn't look how you'd expect a female driver to look. She was tiny and put together.'*

She looked back at Maggie's retreating figure and shrugged her shoulders. When she got to the Husky, she'd go inside and have a coffee. Noelle hoped to learn what happened and who the cops planned to talk to. She saw the clerk who was dating Candice's brother when she entered. Noelle thought the girl looked a little green around the gills and hoped she'd be ok.

SHE SAT at an empty table in the corner so she could watch the door and the road. She felt safer having her back to the wall. It prevented someone from sneaking up on her, like a jealous wife. It had happened once, a long time ago, and she still carried the scar on her shoulder where the fork penetrated her skin. Now she'd learned to be more cautious.

She took her time sipping her coffee, enjoying being able to eavesdrop on the surrounding truckers. She would settle in for what would be a long day. There were a couple of officers at the table in the back corner. She wondered if that's where they planned to do their questioning. She couldn't imagine them taking all the drivers over to police headquarters. It would be unreasonable. But if they didn't start interviewing them soon, the drivers would get angry. She could already tell they were getting frustrated and restless.

Noelle had experienced firsthand how important their time schedules were after her travels to the east coast over the summer. She peered up as one of her regulars walked in and made his way over. He plopped down in the seat across from her and offered to buy her another coffee for her company.

She'd enjoy having the company, and it added legitimacy to her presence there. Now she could ask the questions she was dying to ask and get all the details. She leaned back as he filled her in on everything he knew.

DETECTIVE TATE

Detective Tate arrived at the RCMP detachment when a
call came in that they'd found the body of a trucker at the
local Husky. Colby was in the area following up on a lead from a
case five years ago. His pulse raced when the locals suggested it
could be the work of the serial killer. Colby grabbed his files and
hopped in with another officer to head to the crime scene. He smiled
at the thought that this would be the first fresh crime scene, with the
body still in place that he'd be able to examine and could be the work
of the serial killer. The local police had locked down the area as soon
as they arrived, and he had a full truck stop of potential suspects and
witnesses to interview.

The first thing he noticed as they pulled up was the crowd of
onlookers. He rubbed the back of his neck. He wondered why the
officers on scene didn't push them further back? Then he noticed the
tarp-covered body was still on the ground but without proper barricades, and cursed with mixed emotions. The body's presence would
allow him his first opportunity to view the evidence first hand, but it
was hard to keep people with cell phones from taking and posting
pictures. At least they'd cordoned off the area between the two
trucks in order to gather evidence. He realized they were waiting for

him so that the coroner could take the body. He didn't want to waste any time getting from the cruiser to the scene, so he hopped out and strode there with purpose.

Colby looked up at the sky and breathed a sigh of relief that it was a bright sunny day, unlike the typical rain Chilliwack had this time of year. The overcast sky earlier looked like it might rain, but it had since cleared up. Rain would have impeded their investigation and washed away any trace evidence, making their job more difficult.

"Hey, can someone move the gawkers back from the crime scene? I need the area between the trucks covered. Then we can gather the evidence and release the body." He barked at a rather young-looking officer.

He overheard someone from the crowd mutter, 'This must be the dude they've been waiting for. We'll finally get the fuck out of here.'

Colby sighed. He'd need to speak to everyone parked here and to the clerk who called 911. The first person he'd speak to was the man who discovered the body. He spoke with an officer and told her to hand out numbers to the truckers so they'd be ready for the interview process.

THE CORONER REMOVED the body and took it to the morgue. They'd bagged the evidence and sent it off to the lab. The killer had slashed the victim's neck just like the others, and they'd also found the child's hair clip near the body. They knew it was the work of their killer. Now Colby needed to begin the tedious task of interviewing everyone.

He commandeered a table in the back corner of the restaurant and waited. Soon, an officer escorted the first witness. The man who'd discovered the body and whose truck they'd used to block the mob from watching the evidence gathering process. He checked his notes for the man's name as he approached. Henri Tremblay.

He observed the tiny man, who appeared jittery. Colby guessed by his mannerism that he wasn't the killer. His ashen face said it all, and he fiddled with a package of cigarettes, turning it over and over in his hands.

Colby stood up as Tremblay reached the table, with his hand outstretched, and introduced himself.

"Hello Henri, I'm Detective Tate. I'm conducting the interview. I understand you are French Canadian. Will you need an interpreter?"

Colby took Henri's limp hand, who shook his head.

"Et es fine. I speak both, but French es ma preference." Colby smiled. He was fluent in both languages, but preferred to interview in English. At least he could understand Henri, even if his pronunciations weren't clear. This was the first of many interviews. So, he settled himself in for what would be an endless day.

60

RYAN

*R*yan took his time as he made his way to Maggie's group after chatting with Krissy. He carried a small piece of paper clutched in his hand. He knew he'd end up stuck here for another day, and time would pass quicker with Maggie's crew, but he wanted to see if they'd cleaned up the crime scene.

"Hey." He greeted Josh and JD as he approached. "Where's Maggie?"

"She left on one of her grocery hikes," JD laughed.

"Grocery hike?" Ryan asked.

"Ya. Maggie takes her old lady bundle buggy and walks around town, gathering stuff for supper. She won't just head to the Superstore. She likes the meat from Fraser Valley. Plus, I think she was getting some wine."

"She's been gone an hour already, so she should be back soon." Josh cut in. "I see you picked up your number." He finished motioning to the piece of paper in Ryan's hand. Ryan nodded.

"Ya, a cop came by with ours. I've got Maggie's, seeing as she was out walking when they came around to give us our interview order. They're going to move things along as quickly as they can. The cops understand they are holding up the drivers. They have all of our contact information if they need to get in touch with us in the future. I think the interviews are going to be short. Not that it matters to us. We're still here a few more days." JD smiled.

"I guess I should be happy. The number they gave me was 10. I think the cops based the numbering on how close you parked to the body."

"Well, that makes sense, then. We've got 33, 34, and 35." Josh chuckled. "Come sit down while we wait for Maggie."

They made their way to the trailer and climbed in. They sat in the chairs that were still in place from the previous night and continued chatting. Ryan tucked the piece of paper with his number on it in his pocket and made himself comfortable.

His chance meeting with Maggie that day she helped him with his tarp had turned out to be a blessing, especially on longer than regular stopovers like this one. He liked the group of guys he'd met from her company and wondered if they were hiring any more company drivers. Driving enclosed vehicle transport seemed like a sweet deal.

61

FRANK

rank looked at the piece of paper the cop gave him. Number 26. He cursed under his breath before crumpling it into a ball and shoving it into his pocket. He wanted to get moving, and soon. It pissed off his dispatcher when he told them what happened in Chilliwack and that he couldn't go anywhere until he spoke to the investigating officer. Being stuck here wasn't part of the plan. He was lucky they couldn't search his truck without a warrant. He didn't want anyone to see his souvenirs.

Frank ambled back to the restaurant. He ate his breakfast, and now it was lunchtime. It sounded like he'd be having all three of his meals at the Husky. He should change it up and walk across the street to Wendy's, but didn't relish the extra steps.

When he looked inside the restaurant, he found that all the tables were full. The only ones empty were those in the cordoned off area. He cursed again. He guessed his only choice was Wendy's, unless he wanted to wait, which he didn't. 'What a pain in the ass this is!' He thought to himself.

He walked out the front door just as that skittish girl he bumped into this morning walked by, rolling a cart behind her. Frank noticed her eyes widened when she recognized him. He sensed he'd scared her, but he couldn't figure out why. There was no way she knew anything about him. Frank wondered if it was his appearance and looked down at himself. As he did, his belt buckle caught the sun and flashed. She stopped dead, turned and looked at his buckle. Her eyes widened, then she hurried away. He figured she must have daddy issues. Although if he had kids, she'd be closer to the age of a grandchild.

He tried to ignore her and continued on his way. Frank didn't want to draw attention to himself, and if anyone noticed how she reacted to him, someone might ask questions. He crossed with the lights and made his way to the Wendy's, trying to forget the young woman. He considered his options at Wendy's and thought maybe he'd get some chilli cheese fries with his meal. The burgers were small, so he'd need to buy two.

FRANK LEANED back in his chair when he finished eating and watched a mother enter with two little tow-headed girls. He grinned at their sweet cherub faces.

"Hello, pretty ladies." He called out as they passed where he sat.

The mother gave him an odd glance. One girl moved closer to her mom, while the other stopped to stare at him. 'She's perfect.' He thought, as she smiled back at him. Until her mother grabbed her arm and tugged her along.

A scowl crept across his brow.

'Stupid bitch,' he cursed. 'I did nothing wrong. Hell, I kinda look like Santa Claus, without all the red clothing.'

Frustration boiled under the surface. How dare the mother react that way! All he did was say hello. Frank kicked back his chair, got up, and left. He'd faced enough judgements for one day. He needed a nap, and it would help pass the time until it was his turn to talk to the RCMP detective.

62

DETECTIVE TATE

olby sat at the table in the back corner of the Husky restaurant with a fresh cup of coffee in front of him. The location wasn't ideal for conducting initial interviews, but it would give him a starting point. He'd be able to get in contact with anyone from their list at a future date if he needed to. He glanced down at the number 10 on his witness list and waited for the next person. Colby looked up as a tall reed of a man approached. He had his hand stretched out in greeting. He looked down at the name beside the number and stood. Ryan Walker.

"Hello, you must be Ryan Walker. I'm detective Tate. Please have a seat." Colby noticed his grasp was firm.

"I'm not sure how I can help. I was inside the building when the guy who found him came in. It wasn't until he spoke that I found out someone died."

"That may be true. But you can verify the condition he was in."

"Yes, I can do that."

"Can you describe to me what happened and what you know?"

"Sure. I just got out of the shower. I was planning on getting an early start on my day when this guy burst into the store with his hands covered in blood."

"He had blood on his hands?" Detective Tate questioned.

"Yes."

"Did you think he may have done something when you saw the blood?"

"No way. He was staring at his hands in horror, as if they didn't belong to him. He was screaming something in French and for the cashier to call 911." Ryan finished, and ran his hand through his hair.

"Then what happened?"

"She called 911, and the man entered the washroom. I followed him. He went to wash his hands, but I told him not to. I told him it might make him look suspicious if he washed the blood off. I figured he had blood on him because he touched the body. The cops would figure it out. He thanked me. I can say he looked green around the gills. For a moment I thought he was going to puke."

THE QUESTIONING CONTINUED for a few more minutes before Colby felt Ryan had told him everything he knew. Most of the witnesses wouldn't be able to help, but it was protocol. Ryan corroborated Henri's version of the events. He took down Ryan's contact information in case he needed to ask him any more questions, dismissed him and moved onto the next potential witness.

DR. COLEMAN

*A*udrey sat at her desk, making notes in the file of her last client. Her day was over and she was eager to get home when the phone rang. She looked at the call display and saw that it was 156 and hesitated. Her work day was over and it was after hours. She could feel the tension in her neck and shoulders. She stifled a yawn. There had been so many calls from 156 in recent weeks. In her heart, Audrey realized something was wrong. She reached over and picked up the receiver.

"Hello, 156."

"Hello, Dr. um... Audrey."

"Is everything ok?"

"Have you heard the news about the latest murder victim in BC?"

Audrey hesitated. She hadn't listened to the news in a few days. She found it depressing, and it was coming up to the anniversary of Sara's death. Maybe this was the call she'd been expecting, the call that revealed that 156 was going to admit to knowing who the serial killer was.

"No 156. I haven't had the news on for a few days. Tell me what's going on."

"They discovered a body this morning in Chilliwack. I'm parked here at the very truck stop where they found him. They've shut the whole parking lot down while a detective from the RCMP interviews everyone. I've never been so close when a body was found." 156's voice lowered to a whisper with the last sentence.

Audrey startled at the tone in 156's voice and wondered if she detected a hint of fear. The only thing she could think of was to suggest that 156 needed to use the coping mechanisms they worked on during therapy.

"156, are you ok?"

"Yes."

"Ok, then listen to me. You need to go for a walk and clear your head. Traumas like this can generate flashbacks. Focus. You can't change what you're facing, but you have the tools to deal with it."

"I know Audrey, I just... well... I wanted to hear your voice. After everything we've been through together, you can help me face what's ahead." The voice belonging to 156 sighed.

"Ok. You did the right thing. I've told you to call me anytime. I'll always be here for you."

"Thanks, Audrey. I've got to go. It's almost my turn to talk to the detective, and I'll take your advice and stretch my legs first."

"Anytime. If you need to talk, call me after you've spoken with the detective. Use my cell. I'm heading home after we hang up."

Audrey placed the phone back in the cradle and stared at the picture of Sara and Rick on her desk. So much had happened since their deaths. 156 resonated with her more than any other client. It wasn't her first case, but it was her most memorable. She hoped the killings had nothing to do with 156. But based on the typology of the victims, it wouldn't surprise her.

She put the file she was working on away in the filing cabinet and headed for home. She suspected she was in for a long night, so she grabbed some takeout and a bottle of wine on her way.

DETECTIVE TATE

olby moved down the list of witnesses. Most of the truckers would have been asleep and not seen anything. But he had to interview them all to eliminate them as potential suspects. Then he'd clear the lot so that the drivers could leave. He was already feeling the heat from above. The drivers had to get moving. The investigation was holding up commerce.

He looked up at the burly, grizzled man who approached him and checked his name on the list: Frank Carter. His appearance was what Colby expected a typical trucker to look like, from his protruding stomach, long grey beard, and a big metal Mack belt buckle that was holding up his well-worn jeans. Right away, he could tell Mr. Carter needed a shower. *Why didn't he take advantage of the waiting time to do so?'* He wondered to himself.

"Hello, Mr. Carter. I'm Detective Tate. Please have a seat." This time, he didn't offer his hand. There was something off-putting about the man in front of him. It had nothing to do with the foul stench emanating from him, but something about his demeanour, Colby couldn't put his finger on it.

"Bout fuckin' time!" Frank grumbled as he dropped into the seat across from Colby.

"Yes, I'm sorry the process is taking longer than you'd like, but I'm sure the victim didn't plan on dying, either." Colby couldn't resist letting his annoyance with Carter's attitude show.

Frank cast his eyes down at the table and, under his breath, he mumbled something that sounded like an apology. But Colby couldn't be sure. So, he began the interview.

"According to my notes, you parked your truck in the row behind the victim. Can you tell me what time you arrived and what your movements were?"

"Am I a suspect?" Frank fired back.

"Everyone and no one is a suspect at this point. What I'm trying to understand is the timeline. When you arrived, was anyone around? Did you go into the store, walk past the victim's rig, anything?"

"Oh. Ok then. Well, I pulled in about 10 last night. A lizard climbed outta a truck two down from the Frenchie."

"Lizard?"

"Ya. Lizard, you know, lot lizard, working girl, hooker!"

"OK." Colby made some notes, and Frank leaned closer to see what he was writing. Colby shifted his body to prevent Frank from seeing what he jotted down and said, "Please continue."

"Ya, well, the lizard got out and hopped on her bike. I didn't look where she went. I stepped out and took a piss, then headed to bed. Other than her, I saw no one." Frank leaned back. "I didn't realize someone got killed until I got up this mornin' and noticed the mob."

"This 'lizard'. Do you know where she is?"

"Ya. She's sittin' over there." Frank turned and pointed towards a table with three people at it. Two drivers and a dark-haired woman.

The woman turned and looked their way. Colby motioned to the officer standing beside him and asked him to collect her. He wanted to speak with her next, even if it was breaking protocol.

HE CONTINUED QUESTIONING Frank for a few more minutes before letting him go. Colby noticed Frank was hostile and not forthcoming.

He jotted down some notes before the girl arrived. This working girl might be the first actual witness they had. It's possible she saw something to help with his investigation. He was going to squeeze her in before seeing the next driver.

65

NOELLE

$\mathcal{N}$oelle sat with two of her regulars enjoying a coffee when the burly trucker headed to the back, where the detective was interviewing everyone. She remembered him from last night. He'd wanted a BJ. He was the second last customer she'd serviced before heading home. It had already been over two hours since she arrived and hoped they'd get to her soon. No one had given her a number, but she knew it wouldn't be long before someone told the cops who she was and they'd get to her. Noelle breathed out a deep sigh, thankful to have had the company while she waited. She knew her softened appearance had something to do with it. People didn't want to sit around talking to working girls or girls who looked like working girls.

Out of the corner of her eye, she saw the burly guy turn and point in her direction. The detective leaned to the left to look at her. She turned to be sure and her heart sank. She knew he'd said something about her and wondered what it was. Her companions were so deep in their conversation they failed to notice that they were being watched.

She saw the detective lean over and speak to the officer who stood beside him. It wasn't long before the officer approached their table.

"Hello, Miss. Detective Tate wants a word with you as soon as he's finished with that guy." The officer said, motioning to the rear table with a jerk of his thumb.

"Um, sure," Noelle replied, swallowing hard. She knew it was coming, but her gut clenched anyway. Everyone here knew she worked the lot. It was only a matter of time. It surprised her that it took so long for someone to point her out. She turned in her seat so she could watch for the trucker to leave and take his place with the detective.

66

DETECTIVE TATE

*W*hen Frank left, he motioned for the other officer to bring the working girl over. Colby stood up to greet her. He didn't care what she did for a living. He'd still show her respect. If he didn't, his grandfather and father would've knocked him down a peg.

"Hello, Miss. I'm Detective Tate. Please take a seat."

She took his outstretched hand before introducing herself.

"Hi, I'm Noelle Tucker." She replied as she settled into the proffered chair.

"It's my understanding that you frequent this Husky." Colby began. On registering the hesitation on her face, he interjected, "I know what you do for a living. I'm not worried about that. I'm more concerned about what you might have seen last night."

Noelle bit at her lip. Cops made her nervous, no matter what they promised. What she did was illegal, although one of the oldest professions. She'd even serviced a cop or two when she first started out in the business.

"I 'visited' a few special friend's last night." She looked up at Detective Tate, waiting for his reaction. Instead, he motioned for her to continue. "I left the lot around 11 pm last night. I didn't see anyone around."

"Someone told me that the last truck you visited was parked two trucks away from the victims."

"Do you mean the guy who just left?" Noelle asked.

Colby nodded.

Noelle chuckled. "Yes, I found that out this morning when a friend called me. She was checking in, and told me what happened. When I left, I saw the guy in his cab. His eyes stayed focused on his tablet. I assumed he had porn on the screen, because I could tell he was whacking off. I remember thinking that he could have used my services, but I just continued home." She replied, running her fingers through her hair.

"What made you look at him?"

"Well, I lock my bicycle to the dumpster so that no one steals it. The guy's truck faced forward. When I unlocked my bike, I looked up, and saw him."

"Did anyone catch your attention? Maybe another trucker with lights on nearby?" Colby scribbled some notes in his book.

"No. Both rigs on either side had their curtains closed, and the interior lights were off. There was a truck at the pumps getting fuel. I don't know who. I wouldn't have a clue if anybody in another row was awake. After a busy night, I went home. Didn't the last guy you spoke to mention I visited his truck too?" She finished with a satisfied smirk.

Colby couldn't hide his surprise. Carter left that little detail out. If he omitted telling him he used the services of this working girl, what else wasn't Carter telling him? He could tell by the smirk on Noelle's face she knew she gave him information he didn't have. At least she was local. If they needed to speak to her again, she wouldn't be hard to find.

COLBY ASKED her a few more questions. In the end, he felt he had all the information he needed. He made a note to check the victim's search history. What kind of porn would he watch? The method of kill fits the victimology. If he were a betting man, he'd lay odds on it being child porn. So far, the connection between the victims appeared to be deviant behaviour towards children. It was possible a vigilante was committing the crimes. He hoped the tech guys would have the answer when he finished up here.

Colby watched Noelle leave. She turned to her companions and said, "I'll catch up with you later." She picked up her purse, slung it over her shoulder, and left the restaurant.

67

MAGGIE

*M*aggie and JD sat at a table waiting for Josh to finish speaking with the Detective. Maggie was up next, and after her, it was JD's turn. She took a sip of her coffee and glanced at her phone to check the time. Maggie's hand trembled, and she put the cup down with a clatter. At least she'd have time to go for a walk when this was over. That way, she could clear her head before getting supper on, as long as the interview went well. She frowned as she thought to herself. JD's eyebrows raised when he noticed her frown, so she smiled, allowing herself to think of the bacon-wrapped pork medallions she had for tonight's BBQ.

There weren't many drivers left to interview, which meant they'd be opening up the exits to the flood of drivers eager to leave. She assumed Ryan would be one of them. She felt a special bond with him and hoped to one day meet his family. The story he told everyone in the trailer the other day cinched it. One day soon, Maggie would call him and tell him all about it. She smiled at the possibility of letting him know what a good man she knew he was.

Maggie was so lost in her thoughts; she didn't hear what JD said. She just noticed the odd way he looked at her. Maggie blushed and peered up at him.

"Sorry, JD, I missed what you said."

"What were you thinking about? I could tell you were a million miles away. You know there's nothing to worry about, right? We were all together last night."

Maggie chuckled. "Meeting with the detective doesn't worry me. I was just thinking how glad everyone will be when the Detective finishes his interviews. I can visualize the stampede of trucks heading for the exits."

JD threw back his head and laughed out loud. His deep baritone laughter caused several heads to turn in their direction.

"Well, at least we won't get tangled in that mess. We have a few more days before we leave."

"Yes, there's no hurry. When I'm finished with the Detective, I'm going to take a walk and clear my head. I'll return in plenty of time to start the BBQ."

"Another walk? You keep this up, and you'll disappear. Soon there'll be nothing left of you." JD teased.

"You're a jerk." She smirked, smacking at his hand.

"Seriously, is there anything we can do? Maybe some prep?"

"Thanks, JD, but I already did it. Maybe you can set up the BBQs. Oh, and have an ice-cold beer ready for me." Maggie finished with a wink. "I'll be craving one when I get back from my walk."

"Done."

They noticed Josh stand up to leave. Now it was Maggie's turn, so she stood up and made her way to the back of the restaurant where the Detective was.

68

DETECTIVE TATE

Colby watched the petite, pretty blonde as she headed his
way. She didn't look like a trucker, so he checked his notes
to see. Yes, here it was, Maggie Hopkins. She drove with the same
company as Josh, the driver he just finished interviewing.

When she was within range, he stood up to introduce himself.
With his hand outstretched, he said, "Hello, Miss Hopkins. My
name's Detective Tate. Please have a seat."

He paid attention to her firm grasp before she plopped herself
down on the chair across from him. Her full smile revealed even
white teeth. With her blonde hair, he expected to see blue eyes but
found the wide jade ones that stared back at him, surprising. He
fumbled with his papers for a moment while he pulled himself
together and began.

"I'm sure you know that I'm talking to all potential witnesses that
were parked here and may have information regarding last night's
crime." He waited while she nodded.

"Can you tell me what you were doing between midnight and
three am?"

She leaned back and smiled before responding.

"Midnight and three? I was sound asleep. We had a bit of a

trailer gathering. Several other drivers and myself had a potluck dinner. We set up a bunch of chairs in my empty trailer and consumed a few beverages, if you get my meaning."

"How can you be sure of the time frame?"

"Because one of the drivers got a phone call. We noted it was 11:30 and packed it in for the night. Josh and JD, they're with the same company that I am, walked with me up to the washrooms. They get a little protective of me." She chuckled. "Anyway, we said good night and climbed into our respective rigs. I had my curtains closed and lights out by midnight."

"I see. Did you know the victim? Maybe you saw him when you went to the building and, if so, did he stand out in any way?"

Maggie hesitated. She didn't want to speak ill of the dead. But there was something. Sensing her hesitation, he encouraged her to speak.

"If you know something, you need to tell me whatever you can. Maybe you saw something. Whatever it is, it may help us find whoever did this."

"You're trying to connect this to the other dead truckers, aren't you? I heard there's a serial killer working along the highway." Maggie cut in.

"I can't talk about an ongoing investigation. Please answer my question."

"Well... I noticed the guy who got killed was awake when we walked out of the washrooms." Maggie paused and brushed her hair behind her left ear. "He was looking at his tablet. The only reason I noticed him was that his truck was facing the building, and it was the only one with a light still on."

Colby's ears picked up, and he thought, 'that working girl. What was her name again? Oh, ya Noelle, that's it. She mentioned the same thing.'

"Did you get a glimpse of what was on the screen?"

"No. I didn't get that close. Is it significant?" Maggie questioned.

'She's a smart one.' Colby thought before continuing. "Anything you can tell us is important."

THE QUESTIONING CONTINUED for a few more minutes before Detective Tate felt satisfied. He had enough information from her. He felt certain she saw nothing and dismissed her. When she left, he couldn't help but watch and admire the sway of her hips. Colby twisted the wedding band on the third finger of his left hand. He needed to head home for a few days and see his wife.

69

RYAN

*A*fter his interview with the detective, Ryan took a walk before he went back to his truck to call his wife. He listened to it ring, waiting for her to pick up.

"Hey baby, I love you today!" He chimed in as soon as she answered. He could almost hear the smile that crept onto Krissy's face.

"I love you today. What's happening? Did you speak with the detective? Are they opening the lot and letting you leave?" Her words rushed out.

"That's why I'm calling. The cops just finished all the interviews. A tow truck has removed the truck that belonged to the dead guy, and they've opened the exits. I'm ready to roll."

"Oh baby, I'm so happy. The sooner you get out of Chilliwack, the better." Krissy sighed with relief. "My stomach has been in knots ever since you told me about the murder. It could have been you!"

"No, it couldn't, Krissy. There are rumours that all the murder victims are pedophiles. I'm no pedophile."

"Oh, my god! How do you know? What have you heard?"

"Someone overheard the cops saying that the victim was

watching kiddie porn just before the killer murdered him and that it matched the pattern. I don't have the details, but based on that, I'm safe." Ryan reassured her. "Listen, I'll be leaving soon. I have my dispatch and I'm ready to take off. I'm just going to grab a coffee and say goodbye to the others and then I'll be on my way."

"Good. Any idea of when you'll be home?"

"My delivery is in Toronto, and then I'll head back to the yard. So, I'll be home after that maybe four or five days depending on the weather. I want to get moving, so I'll call you later. Love you, Babe."

"I love you too."

Ryan disconnected the call and put his phone back on the charger. Before he left, he wanted to say goodbye to Maggie and her crew. As he walked across the parking lot, he noticed the French man had left. Ryan didn't blame him. If he'd found a body, he'd want to leave as soon as possible too. As it was, he couldn't wait to put some miles between Chilliwack and himself.

He saw Maggie standing in front of her rig, and she waved to him as he approached.

"Hey Ryan, did you get a load?" Maggie asked.

"Sure did." A smile a mile wide split across his face. "As much as I've enjoyed your company, I'll be happy to get out of here."

"That's great! I'm glad they got you a load." JD cut in. "I can't wait to get out of here, too. I think we're leaving in the morning. We could stay a few more days, but with everything that's happened, it's time to go."

"Well, I came to say goodbye and thank you for the hospitality." Ryan finished, reaching his hand out to shake those of Josh and JD.

He turned to Maggie and hugged her. "Now you take extra care out there. Call me when you want to chat or if you need anything. Krissy said to thank you for ensuring I got fed." He grinned as he looked down at her.

Maggie blushed. "It's what we do. We take care of our fellow brothers and sisters on the road. We're family."

Ryan nodded as he responded. "Anyway, we will run into each other again soon. Be safe."

Ryan headed to use the washroom and grab a coffee before he left. The slight delay of saying goodbye would allow the lineup of trucks to leave.

70

FRANK

rank's body sagged in his seat. He couldn't believe he was on the move again and putting distance between himself and this whole mess. This investigation thing was a pain in his ass. If he'd had enough hours, he'd have continued down the road straight to the next available truck stop last night. But he'd pulled into the Husky and got delayed because of a body. It was just his luck.

He wheeled his rig along the back row as he headed towards the exit. In the corner, he spotted a small group of drivers gathered. Including the stuck-up bitch who made a scene when he said hello. *'Good riddance.'* He muttered as he went past.

He turned his head and took one last look at them, then noticed she was staring at him. It was almost like she knew all of his secrets. But that was ridiculous. There was no way she could know. He saw her take her phone out of her pocket and take a picture of his truck and trailer as he went by.

'What the hell was that about?' He wondered. He shook his head, figuring she was trying to piss him off.

He reached up for his CB.

"Hey, can anyone tell me what the Coquihalla is like right now? I'm heading East."

The crackle of static broke through. Then he heard the voice.

"It's all clear. Sunny with dry roads ahead." The driver responded.

"Thanks, I appreciate it."

He placed the mic on the receiver and turned his wheel to take the on-ramp to the highway. He was back to what he enjoyed; driving the open highways in silence.

71

MAGGIE

The parking lot cleared out at a rapid pace. Maggie couldn't believe how fast they went from full to empty. Now only a handful of trucks remained, most of which were the car haulers. She, JD, and Josh spent the day cleaning out their trailers, so they'd be ready to head to Vancouver in the morning and pick up the cars from the convention centre.

Maggie folded up the chairs and tucked them away in the trailer. Setting the ones that didn't belong to her outside the door for their owners to pick up. Maggie placed her chair in between the bars at the side of the trailer and secured it with a small bungee cord. The small folding camp table she travelled with slipped in behind the chair. She placed Josh's BBQ in the doorway so he could pick it up and stowed hers up in the trailer's nose. Then she swept the inside of the trailer out.

When Josh came by, he saw she was sweeping, so he took his BBQ and chairs and put them away. Tonight, they were planning on walking down to the White Spot on Luckakuck Way for supper, so they wouldn't need the BBQs.

They had an early morning ahead of them, so they planned on

returning to their trucks to get a good night's sleep. There would still be more BBQs ahead of them.

Maggie liked this truck stop for the conveniences, but this experience left her feeling uneasy. Bodies, cops, and a sense of distrust that still lurked in the parking lot. The sense of mistrust hid behind every shadow, just out of sight, knowing this made her happy to be leaving. The next time she was here, she may have to carry her army knife to protect herself. She didn't like it. What bothered her wasn't just the murdered victim; it was the crazy man who chased her with a knife. That was a close call. She didn't know what would have happened if JD hadn't been there.

WITH THE TRAILER CLEANED, she locked the doors and stepped up to her cab to grab her travel bag. It was a good time to shower. Better to get clean before supper. They'd be leaving too early in the morning to worry about getting one then, and she wanted to look nice when they went out to eat.

She knew JD and Josh wouldn't be far behind her once they finished cleaning their trailers. At least she'd have time to go back to her truck and dry her hair. *'Maybe she'd surprise the boys and put a little makeup on,'* she thought with a smile.

BRIGHT AND EARLY THE next morning, they made their way to Vancouver to load the cars. The downtown core was a snarl of traffic surrounding the convention center and it was slow going. JD and Josh worked together with her to ensure they were all loaded before anyone left.

Now that she had the cars back on her trailer, Maggie left Vancouver and began the trip back east. JD and Josh had gone on ahead and took the Fraser Valley to Edmonton. They each had a car to drop at a dealership along the way. Maggie had a straight trip back to the yard. She loved driving this early in the morning, when the traffic was light.

She passed through Sicamous as the sun peaked on the horizon. Once she was through Sicamous, she noticed another rig ahead of her on Highway 1, and her heart sank. From this distance, she knew who the truck belonged to. She pushed down on the accelerator to gain speed and try to catch up with it. There was no way she was letting him out of her sight, not again. Her palms were sweating as she closed the distance between them. She couldn't overtake him on this stretch of highway, but she could still be a nuisance. She pulled right up behind him and used her moose bumper to give him a little push, smiling as she did.

72

NOELLE

*N*ow that the cops had cleared out of the Husky, Noelle felt free to offer her services again. She spiked up her hair and added some kohl around her eyes before grabbing her bicycle and heading out.

Noelle wheeled her bike into the parking lot and noticed that the car haulers had left, and she breathed out a sigh of relief. She no longer had to avoid the back corner.

When she rode into the parking lot, she noticed that only a few trucks peppered the lot. It was unusual for the place not to be almost full at this time of the day. She assumed some truckers avoided the Husky. Not that she could blame them. Someone was killing truck drivers, and that person had been in Chilliwack only a few days ago.

Candace had called again and suggested Noelle take a few more days off. Being around a trucker right now might prove dangerous to her health. Noelle just laughed it off. She could take care of herself, plus she doubted the killer stuck around. She figured whoever it was would have been long gone before they found the body.

Noelle circled the parked trucks, letting them know she was available. Having her as a distraction would keep their minds off what had happened. It wasn't long before someone signalled her over and after a brief negotiation; she locked up her bike and climbed in, ready to start another night of work.

KEDROSTLOW

...and he opened. It wasn't long before ... for over... and after a good nap ... she looked up for ... and ... re... ... to ... a ... of work.

73
_____

DETECTIVE TATE

Colby rubbed the back of his neck with his lips pursed as he looked at the pile of interviews notes. They still didn't have any leads to reveal the identity of the killer. The investigation had stalled out. They had been tight-lipped about their suspicions on how the killer picked his target, but somehow, the information got out. In one of his interviews, a man had commented that the victim was a pervert and even suggested the killer did the world a favour. The one piece of evidence they'd kept to themselves was the hair clip. He had a mountain of evidence but no suspects. The evidence convinced him that their killer had to be another driver. It was the only way their killer could slip in and out of the truck-stop unnoticed. He was positive they were dealing with a vigilante. The common denominator between the victims was a perverted attraction to little girls. He made a note to check the database and see if they had a child attacked by a trucker just prior to the start of the killing spree.

He gathered up the files and stowed them in his briefcase. The BC detachment would send copies of the forensic reports by email to his office in Halifax. He needed a shower and a shave before hopping on the flight back home. His wife told him she wanted to talk to him, and it needed to be in person. He worried about what she meant.

COLBY STOPPED in the office to drop off the files before he headed home. He pulled into his driveway and sat in his car to gather his thoughts. Colby loved his wife but knew his line of work was difficult for her. He took a deep breath before going inside. He hoped she wasn't ending their marriage, but the concept of a face-to-face talk left his stomach in knots.

"Hi honey, I'm home." He called out as he dropped his briefcase by the door. He worried she would tell him she couldn't handle being a cop's partner anymore - a lump formed in his throat.

"I'm in the living room." She purred.

He stopped dead when he walked in. His wife sat on the sofa by a small fire wearing a lacy teddy. Sitting on the table in front of her sat a bottle of sparkling cider and two champagne flutes. The sense of dread ebbed away as another part of his anatomy strained to greet her.

He leaned over and placed his hands on either side of her face to kiss her. He could almost feel her vibrating as he realized she was giddy with excitement. A sense of relief washed over him, thankful that he'd guessed wrong.

"Are we celebrating something?" He asked, as he gathered her in his arms.

"Yes." She replied. Then handed him two white and blue plastic test strips. "We're pregnant."

Colby swung her around with enthusiasm before he pulled her into a deep embrace. His face beamed with pride as he stared down at her still nonexistent belly.

"Baby, this is the best news ever!"

7 4

FINAL

*M*aggie scowled as she rammed the truck in front of her again. The driver struggled to keep it on the road. She'd slammed into it several times with her protective moose bumper, the last time with significant force. It didn't matter how hard she tried; he wouldn't pull over. There was no way he didn't know she was trying to get his attention.

'How stupid can he be?' She wondered. *'If he didn't pull over soon, she'd end up sending him over the edge.'*

One more bump and he'll have to pull over. This cat-and-mouse game needed to end. Unable to hide her frustration any longer, she smacked the steering wheel and cursed. Bang. One more bump. This time, his truck swerved too far to the left. She watched in awe as the trailer leaned over, threatening to take the truck with it. The trailer swung wide, and the truck careened over the edge. Maggie slammed on the brakes and pulled off onto the shoulder. It wasn't her intention to cause him to crash, but he wouldn't pull over. Now he'd suffer the consequences of his actions. She needed him to know she knew who and what he was.

Maggie reached into her side pocket and pulled out her knife. She may need to cut the seat belt and free him before she finished the job. When she freed him, she'd let him know why she chased him down.

Maggie scrambled down the incline to the burgundy and cream Mack truck. The rig landed on its passenger side. The shell of the trailer had torn away, and the contents scattered throughout the gully. She hoisted herself up to check on the driver, not out of compassion, but out of necessity. The seat belt still held his limp body strapped to his seat. She yanked at the driver's door with all her might, using sheer strength and determination to force it open. Maggie knew it was him, the man from the Husky and from so many years ago. She couldn't hide the look of disgust that crept across her face.

Blood from a head wound covered the driver's face. The steering wheel pressed deep into his chest. She heard the rasps from his lungs as he struggled to breathe. His legs, which disappeared under the smashed dash, were out of sight. She couldn't get him out on her own, nor did she want to. She wanted him to suffer and resisted the urge to reach into her pocket and pull out her cell phone to call 911. Maggie could get the police involved, but they'd link her to the crash, and that couldn't happen.

Out of the corner of her eye, she saw something dangling from the roof of the cab behind the driver's seat. It was a ribbon of little girl's hair bows. Her stomach clenched and heaved. There were over two dozen barrettes on the ribbon. Near the top of the collection was a tiny yellow plastic barrette with the name 'Sara' barely legible and a few clips down was a small pink hair clip with ribbons attached and hand-painted initials in black.

The initials MM glared at her from the now faded bow. Her guts rolled. She reached out and stroked the pale, dirty pink ribbon. A tear formed in the corner of her eye, pooling before it rolled down her cheek. She looked down at the driver and saw his shiny Mack belt buckle peeking out from under his massive stomach. She snapped back his head by grabbing his hair to look at his face. Bile rose in the back of her throat. She was sure it was the man who bumped into her in the Husky, but more than that, it was the man that stole everything from her, changed her whole life.

He'd been so close. The detective interviewed him, but for the wrong crime.

She tore down the ribbon and shoved it down the front of her shirt. She spat at him before slamming her elbow into the side of his head. This caused him to stir. He lifted his head and peered at her. "Help me," he pleaded. His eyes widened with recognition. She slid her blade out of its sheath, her eyes filled with hate; she pressed the blade to his throat just as she noticed the pungent smell of spilled diesel fuel. Maggie had an idea, so she withdrew her knife and fastened it in the sheath. She rolled down his window and prepared to climb back down from the cab to the ground.

"Help me, don't leave me," he croaked.

"I'm going to do more than just leave you!" She yelled at him in anger, "you don't recognize me, do you?"

His eyes narrowed as he shook his head. She knew he recognized her as the girl from the Husky, the one that reacted to him in a bizarre way, but he didn't understand her rage.

Maggie pulled the ribbon of hair clips out and shook it in front of his face. His eyes widened as he tried to grab it from her. She snatched it back and held up the faded pink bow with the MM on it for Maggie Mae, her first and middle names.

"Do you remember her?" Maggie spit at him and watched as he gave a slight nod. "I guess I've changed a lot since then. I dyed my hair to hide the natural red. You killed my father! And stole my innocence. You sick bastard! I guess you didn't expect me to survive, that's ok. Nobody did. But here I am. I've been looking for you."

Frank's mouth moved, but no sound came out. His eyes locked onto hers as recognition flickered. Maggie turned and hopped out onto the ground. She paused and plucked the cigarette from behind her ear, slid her daddy's zippo out of her pocket, flicked it and held the flame to her smoke, taking a deep draw on it to create long ash.

"You are beyond help," she mumbled, walking away as she flipped her smoke into the pool of split diesel, feeling the flames warm her back as the fuel ignited before engulfing the cab. His screams permeated the air as she made her way back to her rig. She donned a pair of black leather gloves and reached into the compartment behind her seat. She pulled out a package of long veterinary gloves, a disposable rain poncho still in its packaging, a package of children's pink hair clips, and a long ceramic knife from the compartment. Maggie took these items to the guardrail, paused at the sight of the Mack truck now engulfed in flames, and tossed the items over the edge to mingle with the scattered debris from inside the trailer, but far enough from the flames that the evidence would survive.

She took a deep breath and returned to her cab, climbed up into the driver's seat, and felt a sense of peace wash over her for the first time in twenty years. Maggie reached into her shirt, removed the ribbon of barrettes, and laid them on the passenger seat. She would find out who they belonged to if it took her the rest of her life. The families needed closure. When she could, she'd return the clips to the correct families with a note that the man responsible was dead and suffered in the end.

She lit a fresh cigarette and pulled down the visor to look at the last picture taken of her and her father when she was eight years old. She'd kept it clipped to the visor with a pink ribboned barrette she wore on that fateful day, with the initial MM, matching the one on the cord, and said, "I did it, dad. I stopped him." When she returned to Cobden, she'd go visit his gravesite and bury both hair clips and her past with him.

233

75

EPILOGUE

*M*aggie put a great distance between herself and the accident before she took a chance and pulled off the road and parked. She picked the ribbon of hair clips up from the passenger seat. The image of her father's death flashed before her eyes as her heart ached. Her hands shook as she thought of how many young girl's lives Frank had ruined or taken. Her fingers reached up and stroked the missing space where her hair clip had been, which now joined its mate on her visor. She recognized a second hair clip on the ribbon and knew she had a call to make. Every week she went in for her counselling sessions, sat in the office and looked at the picture of the little girl who'd worn it and knew her mother had waited decades for this call. This clip was pale yellow with the name 'Sara' now almost illegible etched into it. Maggie picked up her phone and made the call. "Hello?"

"Hi, Audrey."

"156! I'm surprised to hear from you so soon."

"You can call me Maggie now."

Silence drifted from the other end of the line before Audrey spoke again.

"Are you sure? You've always maintained this was the best for us both."

"It doesn't matter anymore. I have news." Maggie replied.

"Is this about the serial killer?"

"Yes." Maggie whispered, "there won't be any more killings."

"What?! Why do you say that?"

Audrey tried to buy time and keep Maggie talking. She sensed she wanted to talk, and the timing was perfect as she was between clients.

"I'm holding something in my hands. The man who I took it from is dead."

"Did you kill this person?" Audrey couldn't help herself from asking the question. She had long ago concluded that Maggie was the serial killer. There were too many indications for it not to have been Maggie. But Audrey also knew why she killed.

"No, I didn't kill him. At least not directly. I may have helped end his life, and I didn't prevent him from dying."

"You need to be clearer, Maggie. I don't know what you're talking about."

"Let me describe to you what I'm holding."

After a long pause Audrey replied, "Ok."

"I'm holding a pale-yellow hair clip. There are still strands of dark hair caught in the clasp. There is a name on it. It's faint, but still visible. The name on it is Sara."

Audrey felt her knees go weak. She reached out for her chair before collapsing into it. Her heart raced and her mouth went dry. She struggled, but found the words.

"Is it hers?"

"How many times did I see the one in your office and the picture of Sara beside it? You told me her story when you were trying to help me heal from mine. I didn't forget what you said. How could I forget? I know it's hers. It was the same man. The same man who killed Sara also hurt me and killed my father. I have my hair clip too." Maggie licked her lips before continuing. "But it's bad. He had over two dozen hair clips in his collection."

"I need you to tell me everything." Audrey opened her desk drawer, grabbed the gin bottle, and poured herself a shot.

Maggie told Audrey the whole story. She started with bumping into him at the Husky and her part in the accident, finding the ribbon of hair clips to Frank burning alive in the cab of his truck. She even mentioned the littered clues to the serial killer in the debris at the roadside.

When she finished, both women were crying. Maggie, because she'd caught the man who'd stolen her childhood. Audrey because the man who ruined her life had met his end.

"I'll be in town in a couple of days. I'm stopping at my father's grave, and then I'll come to see you. You should have Sara's hair clip. I'll bring it to you."

It no longer mattered to Audrey if Maggie was the serial killer. Justice was served. Justice for Sara and justice for Maggie.

GLOSSARY OF TERMS

1. APU - auxiliary power unit - also allows the truck to run heat and air conditioning without running the truck.

2. Bob Tailing - is when a driver is only in the cab of the truck without a trailer attached driving on the road.

3. Bunk Heater - a device that can be installed so that the truck can be heated without running the truck all night.

4. Car Hauler - a trucker who hauls cars on an open deck where the cars are visible.

5. Catwalk - The area behind the cab with stairs and a flat area for the truck driver to get up on.

6. CDL - commercial driver's license

7. Dead Heading - tractor is attached to the trailer but the trailer is empty while driving.

8. Department of Transportation or DOT - have the authority to pull drivers over to inspect a truck at the side of the road or at a weigh scale.

9. Dispatch - the people or person responsible for finding loads for the drivers. They set up delivery and pick up times.

10. Electronic Logging Device or ELD - am electronic device

that records the truckers driving time, on duty not driving time and off duty time according to the hours of service.

11. Enclosed - a trailer that hauls cars that are not visual. They often have either a lift gate (which lifts cars from ground level to the lower or upper deck of cars) or ramps to drive cars on to the different decks inside the truck. The decks that the cars sit on are adjustable in height. Cars are strapped to the decks by their tires.

12. Flat deck or flat bed - a flat trailer that is not covered that carries visible cargo. Cargo must be securely strapped to the deck.

13. Hours of Service - the hours a truck driver has to follow. For example, 70 in 7 refers to the fact that a driver can't drive more than 70 hours in 7 days. It is further broken down to 14 hours on duty in a 16-hour window of time per day. During those 14 hours a maximum of 13 hours of driving time. So, if a driver was on duty but not driving for 5 hours. There would only be 9 hours of driving time.

14. Load - the cargo a truck carries to its destination.

15. Lot Lizard - a working girl or prostitute who works truck stops specifically for truckers as clients.

16. On Duty Not Driving - this includes time fuelling up, delivering etc.

17. O/O - owner operator. Often referred to as owner op. A driver who owns his/her own truck and has the truck leased onto another company.

18. Scale - truck drivers are randomly directed to enter a scale to check the weight of the vehicle and the weight distribution per axel.

19. Sleeper Birth - the back of the cab where the driver's bed is located. In a higher cab, there are usually two single bed bunks. Trucker has storage cupboards for their personal belongings. Some are equipped with a refrigerator. Those with and inverter or APU can run a microwave, tv and other small appliances.

REVENGE - TRANS-CANADA
KILLER SERIES BOOK TWO

Maggie struggled to open her eyes, her brain hazed with confusion and uncertainty. The drone of machines whirred through the fog as she fought for consciousness. The unmistakable beep of medical equipment drifted through the misty recesses of her mind. Her nostrils flared, recognizing the aroma of disinfectant that surrounded her.

She rubbed at her eyes, her movements impeded by the tangle of cords attached to her wrists and hands. Her head throbbed with a constant boom that pulsed with a violence that was unending. She shifted her weight and felt a searing sensation in her abdomen, and winced. Maggie slid her hand down, feeling the crisp sheets beneath her touch, moving her hand lower to her swollen bandage covered stomach and the memory flashed. The blare of gun shots, blood, oh so much blood. NO!

"Liam!" she screamed. Her eyes flew open as the memory flooded into her consciousness.

She blinked and looked around the room. In the corner she saw an officer who stood up from his chair at the sound of her strangled scream and the nurse who jogged in with a needle, which she injected into the IV line. The medicine calmed Maggie, and she slumped back onto the pillow as the fog once again clouded her reasoning. She wanted to speak with the officer who walked towards her. She attempted, in vain, to resist the medication that pumped through her veins as she succumbed to the inevitable drug induced sleep.

"Nurse, I needed to ask her some questions about what happened. I'd appreciate if the next time she wakes up, you didn't give her a sedative right away." The officer complained as Maggie slipped back into unconsciousness.

"She was shot. You, of all people, should know that. It's my job to keep her comfortable and to prevent her from damaging her sutures. My responsibility is to my patient first." With that, the nurse turned and left the room.

The officer stared down at the petite woman in the hospital bed. A cloud of burnished copper curls splayed across the pillow. She had a concussion. Swelling had misshapen the whole left side of her face, which was bruised from where it connected to the pavement after the gunman shot her. The doctors had removed a bullet from her abdomen, but her wound had contained skull fragments and brain matter from the other victim.

Then infection set in and they'd kept her sedated to allow her to heal. The officer flipped his notebook, noted that she regained consciousness, closed and put it away. He'd leave word at the front desk for them to call him when she woke up. She didn't need a guard, so he'd head back to the station to see what else they'd found at the crime scene. One thing was for sure; when she woke up, she'd be in a world of hurt.

ACKNOWLEDGMENTS

In order to do research for this book, I travelled in a transport truck from coast to coast several times. My husband is a long-haul truck driver and when I told him my basic idea for this book, he agreed that a coast-to-coast run was what I needed. In order for accuracy, the roads, exits and truck stops are real. This story is a work of fiction. The characters are people I meet in my head while I'm planning out a story. I'm a people watcher, so I may pick up and borrow character traits and mannerism of people along the way, and I may consider my characters 'friends' because I know each of them intimately while I'm writing, but that's it. Some situations and experiences the characters experience are real. I've taken them from things that happened to me, or that I witnessed while in the truck. The truck my husband has is one of the larger ones, but by the time you account for the second fridge and my potty bucket, we can't both be standing in the back at the same time, except for hugs. We took turns getting dressed for the day and again at the end of the day. You really have to get along well with someone to spend so much time together in close confines. Luckily, we enjoy it. I thank my husband, Steve, for all the endless discussions on trucking, rules and regulations and the logistics. Also, for his love and support and belief in me. I also want to thank my daughter-in-law, Chelsie, for her medical advice to help make the more violent scenes believable. Finally, my beta readers, your encouragement, attention to detail and feedback means the world to me.

ABOUT THE AUTHOR

J. E. Friend is an emerging author of crime thrillers. She lives in the beautiful Annapolis Valley with her husband Steve and their dog, Hartley. There she can enjoy the peace and solitude it offers so that she can write, whether in her writing room or on the deck. She has a Bachelor's Degree from Waterloo, where her field of study was psychology. This enables her to get into the mind of a killer when writing.

She is a member of Authors Ink, a writing group in Nova Scotia, comprising published and non-published authors, and for the past few years, she has also been The Municipal Liaison for NaNoWriMo (National Novel Writing Month) for her geographical area. NaNo-WriMo promotes writers with an annual challenge to write 50,000 words in November, which she has won each year since 2017, except for 2021, when she was busy welcoming identical twin granddaughters. She is an active member of the Writers Federation of Nova Scotia where she has reviewed and short-listed emerging authors in several competitions.

Design of Deception was her debut novel in 2020. Redemption is the first book in the Trans-Canada Killer Series, which follows a serial killer across Canada. Watch for Revenge, book two and Reparation, book three, coming soon.

9 781999 119225